MEMPHIS

THREE KINGS
BOOK 2

ALEXANDRIA HOUSE

Pink Cashmere Publishing

PROLOGUE

Memphis

J udge Oliver Baxter, a distinguished looking, seventy-one-year-old Caucasian man known for his thick southern twang, had held his position on the bench for more than twenty years. He was a family man, husband to Gail, his wife of over forty years, and father to three adult sons—Oliver Jr., John-Francis, and Gregory. An avid supporter of such organizations as The Alliance Defending Freedom and the American Family Association, Judge

Baxter was a staunch conservative famous for his no-nonsense style of doling out justice. His supporters revered him and his contributions to both the judicial system and his community. His detractors? Well, they had a tiny problem with the Honorable Oliver Baxter.

He was a racist.

That alone would be bad enough, but he carried his racism and biases with him onto the bench. It was a matter of public record that he sentenced African Americans far more harshly than whites. Being that he ruled in juvenile matters, he was known to ruin many young Black lives before they truly began, handing down sentences widely regarded as overly punitive in relation to the accused's crimes. Add to that, his penchant for patronizing, and subsequently, abusing Black sex workers, and one might begin to see him for what he truly was— a fucking monster. A monster who favored navy blue, off the rack suits and lunches at the country club with his judge cronies, where they laughed and boasted about the last "hard r" they managed to put away for the good of the community, especially their dear, sacred daughters and granddaughters.

Whoever paid three million dollars to have him eliminated obviously saw him as something less than human. They provided The Agency with all the needed information, some so secret and personal that it made me wonder who the client was. His wife? An assistant? It didn't matter. All that mattered to me was that this one target was doubtlessly worthy of my services, maybe one of the worthiest. This elimination was going to be particularly satisfying for me.

Hidden by trees on a hill which overlooked his secret getaway cabin I'd been provided excellent directions to, I waited with my favorite long-range rifle at the ready. I glanced at my darkening surroundings. The woods spooked me, but I knew Jerryn, my right-hand man, had my back. While I watched the judge's cabin, Jerryn watched *me*.

Sighing, I glanced down at my watch. According to information from the anonymous client, when the judge went on these little trips, he always brought a companion, a *paid* companion, and at some point, he would step outside to call his wife and feed her some bull-shit about how the fishing or hunting was going. I was waiting for him to make that call. I needed him outside and unsuspecting. This would be a clean kill. No evidence, no witnesses. No collateral damage.

I hated collateral damage.

But more than that, I hated the possibility of being arrested, so if his companion somehow caught a glimpse of me—although that was highly unlikely—she would have to be eliminated, too. I didn't want to have to do that; I really didn't. But I doubted she'd follow him outside. She'd probably welcome the break from being in his presence. The judge wasn't exactly eye candy. As a matter of fact, he was the exact opposite of anything pleasing to the eye.

When I saw a door open, casting light into the darkness outside the cabin, I lifted my L115A3 and peered through the scope. There he was—the distinguished judge in his bright white t-shirt and tan slacks looking every bit the evil cretin he was as he lifted his cell to his right ear. With my finger on the trigger, adrenaline flooded my body. This? This rush? It never got old. There was something almost poetic about the moments that preceded ridding the planet of some confirmed scum. It was going to be a pleasure to eliminate this demon.

I was laser focused on my target when my vision blurred. Snatching my head back, I blinked fast, a frown creasing my brow. The fuck? With a racing heart, I quickly resumed watching the judge through the rifle's sight. He hadn't moved, his scant lips still working as he most probably lied to his dear embattled and unattractive wife.

"Raja!" Jerryn's voice in my ear was urgent and too damn loud for that earpiece.

"I got it," I murmured in response, my vision clear and hands steady as I aimed my A.R. and took the shot, damn near blasting my target's head off his shoulders.

When the first drop of expected rain hit my arm, I took that as a cue to make my departure, navigating my way through trees and underbrush as the shower intensified. By the time I made it to my waiting vehicle, over a mile from the cabin, I was drenched and more than a little frustrated, but I got the job done.

Just like I always did.

1

Memphis

He was cute. Young, but cute. He was sitting with a group of other men across the room from my perch at the bar, all of them wearing expensive bespoke suits. All were fit and handsome.

Businessmen.

Rich businessman downing drinks and probably debating the current state of economics or politics, anything to avoid going home to their wives and children. I'd killed more than a few assholes like them, prototypes of what was wrong with the world. However, the cutie who'd just sent me a drink wasn't wearing a wedding band. So, maybe...

When he locked eyes with me, I lifted my lemon drop and gave him a smile while mouthing, "Thank you." He, of course, took that as a sign to leave his companions and navigate his way across The Royale's plush lounge to me, sliding onto the barstool next to mine.

"Evan Weeks," he said, proffering me his hand.

I took it, relishing his firm grip. "Dana Stimson," I replied. Yeah, I was considering giving him some pussy, but I definitely wasn't giving this man my real name.

Fuck that.

"It's a pleasure to meet you, Ms. Stimson. Are you enjoying your drink?"

He had green eyes. I didn't notice that earlier. Green eyes, curly hair, and khaki skin. Biracial, maybe?

"I am. Thank you again," I replied.

"You're welcome, beautiful. When I saw you sitting here looking like you're looking? I just had to get your attention somehow. You're gorgeous. Red looks good on you."

I mean, he wasn't lying. So, I smiled and said, "I appreciate your admiration. My parents did a great job on me, didn't they?"

He laughed. "They did!"

I gave him a genuine smile. He seemed nice. I'd eat him alive if he wasn't careful.

"Yeah, so...what are your plans for the rest of the night?" he asked.

Before I could provide an answer, my phone buzzed with a text alert. Glancing at it sitting on the bar, I had to fight not to roll my eyes when I saw who the message was from. Of course, I ignored it.

"I have no plans, unless you intend to make some for me...*and you*," I replied.

Evan lifted a brow, an amused grin adorning his handsome face. "Oh, straight to the point, huh?"

I shrugged. "I'm too old for unnecessary detours."

"Too old? I don't believe that."

"Okay, let's just say I'm old enough."

My phone buzzed again, this time with a call from the texter.

Ignored.

Again.

Evan leaned in close to me, his musky cologne filling my nose. "Old enough to let me get us a room upstairs for the night?"

"Exactly," I affirmed.

I left the bar with Evan, was standing in the Royale's lobby waiting for him to get our room when I felt a heavy presence I was all too familiar with.

My first thought?

Fuck.

"Why you tryna get that motherfucker killed?" The voice came from behind me—deep, gruff, inducing a chaotic mixture of dread and desire inside me.

When I didn't turn around or verbalize a response, he added, "Because I will shoot that nigga dead, right here and right now. Him and any witnesses. Try me if you want to, King."

"What the fuck are you doing here?" I hissed over my shoulder. "You're having me followed *again*?"

"I *absolutely* had you followed since your ass doesn't know how to come home."

"That's not my home, and by the way, fuck you!" I gritted.

"That's what your ass is supposed to be doing right now." Placing his hands on my shoulders, he leaned in close to my ear. "Or are you reneging on our deal?"

I tried to spin around to face him, but he tightened his grip on my shoulders. Still, I said, "I fucking hate you."

"I know, baby. I know. Now, let's go. I need some of that hateful pussy."

"Uh, Dana? Everything okay?" Evan said, approaching me with a key card in hand. Lifting it, he advised, "I got the room."

The asshole behind me reached around my body, snatching the key card from Evan. "You got us a room? Thanks," Mr. Asshole said, his voice dripping with snark.

"What the fuck—" Evan was cut off by a big hand connecting with his chest. The owner of said hand, a huge man I knew as Moody, warned, "You don't want this, not with him," as he opened his old ass Bulls starter jacket—a wardrobe staple for him—revealing a holstered Glock.

Evan wore a look that was somewhere between confusion and anger as his eyes dropped to meet mine.

I could admit that this was fucked up and that I realized the probability of this happening was astronomical, so I felt bad for Evan. I really did; hence, I offered him a sincere, "Sorry."

Then a hand grasped mine and I was led to an elevator while asking, "Damn, are you going to at least reimburse the man for the room?"

Asshole stopped in his tracks and stared at me. At first glance, this man I'd known and hated for more than half my life appeared unremarkable. Was he handsome? Absolutely, but in an understated way —glasses, salt and pepper beard, average build, not particularly tall —but his aura? His presence? It was suffocating and overwhelming and utterly irresistible. When this man walked in a room, the walls vibrated. Hell, I knew he would show up tonight because I could feel him from kilometers away. Nevertheless, I hated him, but I wanted to hate him more. I *needed* to hate him more.

"Am I going to do *what*?" he inquired, a look of astonishment shrouding his face.

"Are you going to reimburse the man for the room you just stole? It's the least you could do since you also stole *me* from him," I said.

He scoffed, "First of all, how the FUCK can I steal what's mine? Second, why the FUCK would I reimburse a man for a room he was going to use to eat a pussy that belongs to me?"

The elevator doors opened, and as he pulled me inside it, I offered, "Bo, he didn't know about you."

"And now he does."

I snatched my gaze from him, fixing my eyes on the now closed elevator doors as the car began to ascend. When we arrived on one of the higher floors, I looked at him to find his eyes pasted to me.

"He got a suite?" I queried.

The asshole smirked. "Hell no. I got one once I knew you were here. This shit?" He held up Evan's key card. "It's for one of the regular rooms. Probably stub your toe on the bed frame the second you enter the room, and you were planning to give that cheap motherfucker some of that good-ass pussy of yours." He sucked his teeth and added, "Damn shame."

I rolled my eyes and followed him out the box, a few steps down the hallway, and into Suite 1628. He damn near jerked me inside, the door still closing when his arms enveloped me and his lips met my neck. A moan left his mouth as he kissed that sensitive spot just above my collarbone, and that sound led to my rapid undoing. There was just something about hearing that level of vulnerability from a monster because in truth, that was what he was. Hell, Bo Pierce was the boogeyman in the flesh, a night terror, and a real-life Freddy Krueger all rolled into one, but right now and in this moment as he held me close to his body, I could feel his heart racing, his breathing harsh with need...for me.

"I fucking missed you," he growled as he lifted his head, his mouth finding mine in an oxygen depleting kiss that burned hot and slow.

Any response I had to offer was muted by the tongue play we engaged in, my own heart pounding with anticipation of what I knew was to come.

He kissed me so deeply that I felt lightheaded in a wonderful, blissful way. Once our mouths parted, I sighed then gasped when he stepped backward a bit, reaching for my nice, very expensive Nina Rapport blouse and ripping it until it hung from me in tatters. Moments later, I was on my knees in the gorgeous bed in that luxurious suite, my clothes on the floor in a pile of ruined fabric. I was practically whining with need, my body vibrating as I waited for my tormentor to fuck me like only he could. He loved making me wait. He got a kick out of torturing me.

I *really* hated this man.

The bed dipped with his weight as he positioned himself behind me, his hands grasping my hips as the head of his thick dick pressed against the opening of my hungry pussy.

"Bo..." I whined.

He slid his right hand up my back to my hair, grabbing a handful of it as he eased inside me, almost making my entire body collapse onto the mattress. He retreated, and this time, plowed into me with enough force to move me up the bed while causing me to smile.

I'd *definitely* pissed him off.

"You like this, don't you?" he grunted as he punished me *and* my pussy. "You like pissing me off and making me fuck the shit out of you! You enjoy it, don't you?"

"Ohhhhh, fuck!" I wailed.

He tightened his grip on my hair, yanking my head backward *hard*. "Answer me, King!"

"Fuck you! I ain't answering shit!" I spat.

"Oh? You're not?" he asked as he slammed into me.

"Hell. Noooooo!"

"Okay." He punctuated that one-word statement with a punitive thrust that almost sent me into the headboard. He fucked me and fucked me and fucked me, not bothering to stop or ease up even as I screamed my way through a mind-numbing orgasm, and when he hit his peak, he crowded my body, hissing into my ear, "Stop playing like this pussy ain't mine before someone gets deleted out this bitch."

DROWSY SEX WAS the best sex, especially with this asshole. Neither of us had recovered from last night. Plus, neither of us slept well in hotels—side effects of our lifestyles and professions. So, groggy didn't come close to describing our current condition as I lay on my back and watched him close his heavy-lidded eyes while sliding inside me and gripping the pillow beneath my head. Closing my own bleary eyes, I fought not to cry out because this? This slow-stroking shit he was doing? It felt too good and too intimate and too real, but there was nothing good or intimate or real about me fucking Bo. It was business, and honestly, it would only ever be business since I despised him, and he didn't give half a fuck about me outside of a bed.

But damn did he feel like heaven.

When I opened my eyes, I found his fixed on my face, something unsettling in them as he lowered his head to kiss me while continuing to deliver measured strokes. Ending the kiss, he stared at me again, that same look in his eyes. I didn't like this shit. Not at all.

So, I murmured, "The fuck are you looking at me like that for?"

His eyes narrowed as he eased back and plowed into me so hard that my titties bounced, smacking against my chin.

Yeah, I thought, *that's more like it.*

"And how the hell am I leaving this place? You fucked up my clothes," I fussed.

"I'll get someone to bring you some got damn clothes. Now, shut up so I can finish fucking you. Shit!"

I did shut up, but not because he told me to. I shut up because I'd accomplished my mission and thwarted whatever declaration of affection his stupid ass was about to make.

Plus, the dick was good.

Shidddd, it was excellent!

2

Memphis

"Hello?" I said into the phone as I stepped out of the elevator. "Lil?"

"Why haven't you been answering your phone? I tried to reach you last night and earlier this morning!" was how my sister replied. "I thought I was gonna have to send Ray out to find you or something! You know you're supposed to let me know when you get back in town!"

Ever since my *younger* sister, Lilith, found out about my profession, she had turned into a damn mother hen or something.

"Lilith, you do realize I'm an adult and I've been doing my job for literal decades, don't you?"

"Whatever. How was your trip?"

"Great. I'm excited to add new products to our offerings at the *FaceCard by Memphis King Day Spa*."

She was silent, but she knew better. We were on the damn phone! I wasn't about to tell her shit about my trip over the phone.

"What was so urgent? I know you weren't just calling to ask about my trip," I continued.

"Oh! I wanted to remind you of the little get together Daddy invited us to. You know we gotta do it potluck-style since Pauline isn't around to do the cooking. Do you know what you're bringing?"

"Something store or restaurant bought, that's for damn sure."

"I figured as much."

I made it down the hall to my apartment to see my front door slightly ajar, and as I reached into the back waistband of the leather pants Bo had bought me and grabbed my gun, I told my sister, "Hey, I gotta go. I'll call you back," and ended the call. Easing the door open, I held the gun up, letting it lead me into my home, and rolled my eyes when I saw Jerryn sitting on the sofa, his long legs stretched out before him.

"You get on my fucking nerves," I gritted as I shut and locked the door.

He smiled. "Just showing you I was right, like I usually am. Security is too lax in this building."

Rolling my eyes *again*, I stated, "Security knows you, negro. *That's* how you got up here."

"Right, but I could be a clone, an imposter."

I stared at him for a moment before saying, "How you can manage to be a goofy ass and a genius at the same time is actually astonishing, and why are you here? I gave you a key to use in case of an emergency."

"This *is* an emergency...of course."

My stomach popped, dropped, and locked it, but my voice was calm and steady as I asked, "What emergency?" Had we made some mistake during the last job? Hell no! We didn't make mistakes.

"Montana and I are concerned about our Raja."

Raja, Swahili for King. My hacker, Montana—not her real name —had given me that nickname. Speaking of my favorite hacker...

"Montana can speak for herself, and why would either of you be concerned about me?" I asked.

"You froze."

Sighing heavily, I dropped into an accent chair, placing my cell and small handbag on the little table beside me. "I didn't fucking freeze. I *never* freeze."

"What would you call it, then?"

"Something that won't happen again."

"It better not. It's not just your life on the line. It's mine and Montana's too."

Through a mirthless chuckle, I reminded him, "*I* pay *you*. It's not the other way around. Therefore, I'll be the one doling out orders and warnings, Jerryn McReynolds. You just do your damn job and stop worrying about me."

He nodded slowly. "You're right, and my job is logistics. I plan this shit down to the second. So, when you let the clock run while you have a perfect opportunity to take the shot, it's going to concern me."

Leaning forward in my chair, I repeated, "Like I already said, it won't happen again."

He stared at me for a moment before standing from the sofa. "Good. I'll look forward to hearing from you when another job comes up."

"Uh-huh...tell your wife I said hi."

He left without uttering another word. I'd hit a nerve...on purpose. He deserved it after tap dancing on all of mine.

Minutes had passed and I was still sitting in that chair when Jerryn texted me: *By the way, nice outfit.*

I glanced down at the leather pants and matching leather tank top that hugged every curve I possessed and rolled my eyes yet again.

He was fucking with me. He knew I wasn't a fan of leather, which told him I didn't purchase this outfit for myself.

Bo Pierce was truly an asshole, so instead of replying to Jerryn, I sent said asshole a text: *Fuck you for buying this outfit.*

Bo: *The sooner the better, baby.*

As I DID EVERY DAY, I got on the Tor browser and logged into The Agency's online portal to see if there was anything in my inbox. There was one message regarding a new assignment. I frowned slightly. This was a faster than usual turnaround, considering the judge's expiration date was just a couple weeks earlier, but fuck it. I never missed an opportunity to do my public service.

According to the attached dossier file, the target was a United States senator. Since this was a rank-and-file member and not the Speaker of the House or someone with a comparable position, there would be no government issued security detail. Granted, they may have hired their own security, but a private firm didn't have shit on the Secret Service. So, this was doable. Add in the generous seven-million-dollar payout and it was *damn* doable. After reading over the particulars and doing a little light internet research regarding the character—or lack thereof—of the target, I quickly accepted the job and contacted both Jerryn and Montana.

3

Memphis

A few days later, I arrived at my father's house with a bucket of fried chicken in tow, still wondering about the purpose of this little shindig. My answer came in the form of the lovely lady who answered the door.

"Candy?" I breathed, quickly mirroring her smile.

"Yes! It's me!" she gushed. "Come in!"

My stepmother's sister-wife had returned.

Wow.

Following her to the kitchen—the usual location for these gatherings—I saw that my sister, Lilith, wore an identical expression to mine. Surprised wasn't the word.

"Chicken?" Lilith asked.

I nodded. "Yup."

"Thank God. You know Denita only cooks healthy shit. She done made some turkey cutlets and asparagus," Lilith said, scrunching up her nose.

Just as I was wondering where my nieces were, my stepmom, Denita, sauntered into the kitchen with the youngest—Katana—on her hip.

"Don't y'all start. You know I'm tryna keep my Frankie alive and well," Denita reminded us.

"Yeah, yeah, yeah," Lilith said, then to Katana she directed, "Look, Katana, it's Auntie Memphis!"

As per usual, the sweet little girl gave me a shy wave and hid her face in Denita's neck.

"Girl, you still acting shy with me?" I cooed.

"She knows evil when she sees it," Lilith's stupid ass husband, Ray, offered as he stepped into the kitchen with Blaze, their oldest daughter. I couldn't stand his ass.

The feeling was mutual.

"Then I know she *stay* hiding from you," I shot back. "Shiddd, she probably already tryna move out."

"She's one, Memphis," Lilith reminded me.

"Exactly," I replied. "Anyway, what did you and Beelzebub bring, Lilith?"

Ray scowled at me. So did Blaze, as always. That girl scowled at everyone. You know, apple...tree.

"We brought a lemon blueberry cheesecake and some barbecue meatballs," Lilith stated.

"Oh, really? You cooked?" Candy chirped. Shit, I'd almost forgotten she was there.

"Girl, no. They got a cook," I shared. "Wait, where's Umber?"

The doorbell rang, and Candy said, "I bet that's her! Let me get the door," and flew out of the kitchen.

"I like how you just assumed I didn't cook the food," Lilith mumbled.

With lifted eyebrows, I asked, "Did I lie, though?"

"Girl, fuck you," Lilith muttered, making me laugh.

"Um, Umber is here, and so is your friend, Memphis!" Candy trilled.

Frowning, I looked up to see my baby sister entering the spacious kitchen carrying a crockpot, and behind her was the asshole, Bo.

4

Memphis

I have GOT to be hallucinating.

I know this motherfucker is NOT standing in my father's house, in his kitchen.

I know good and hell well this nigga did not follow me here and have the audacity to seek entry.

I know the-fuck he didn't have a smirk on his evil-ass face.

Son. Of. A. Fucking. Bitch!

I was so caught up in my thoughts that I initially didn't notice the silence in the room or that all eyes were on me. Ray's were narrowed as they volleyed between me and Bo. I knew he'd never actually seen Bo's face, but he'd been around him; meaning, he was familiar with the goosebumps that usually populated one's flesh when in this man's vicinity.

"Uh...what are you doing here?" I addressed Bo, trying to keep my cool and not scream at his crazy ass.

"You didn't come home. I was worried," he replied.

I didn't look at my family but could imagine them gawking in concert.

I cleared my throat, lifting from my seat at the table. "Uh, let's speak outside," I said, placing a hand on his arm.

His eyes snapped down to my hand before lifting to lock with mine. "Whatever you want, baby."

Without bothering to explain anything to my family, I led him back in the direction he'd come from and out into the front yard. The front door had barely clicked shut when I lit into him.

My voice was low but dripping with venom as I spoke. "What the fuck do you think you're doing? That's my fucking family in there. They are off limits to you, and you know it! This shit isn't part of the deal!" I was in his face, so close that his cologne was assaulting me.

"You didn't come home, King," he bit out. "You haven't been home in weeks. I haven't fucking seen you since The Royale!"

"I *have* been home...at my apartment. You wanna see me, you know the got damn address."

He shook his head, releasing a bitter chuckle. "We've talked about this. I want you in *my* home, in *my* bed every night you're not working."

"We didn't talk about a fucking thing. You said that shit and I ignored it because you don't give me orders!"

"Nice to finally see Lilith in the flesh. She looks happy. She's pretty, too. So is Umber. But you? Oh, baby...you're exquisite. I'm so proud to call you mine."

"Are you threatening my sister? You tryna go back on your word?"

"No, I've kept my word. Your sister is safe. Your brother-in-law left

The Agency with no backlash or consequences. He's walking free with intimate knowledge of the inner workings of my organization. You are still working. You made those demands. I only made one: I get my woman back, *all* of her. I have let this shit go for over two fucking years because that pussy you kept from me for far too long got a little mind control over me. I can admit that." He lifted a hand, placing it on my cheek. "But now, your time is up, my love."

I knocked his hand off my face. "Stop calling me that shit."

"Nope."

"You are a real piece of excrement, Bo Pierce."

"I know, but you like it."

"The fuck I do! Listen, I'll spend three nights a week at your house. Final offer."

He slowly shook his head again. "*Every* night unless you're on an assignment."

"I could kill you, grab my gun while you're asleep and blow your fucking brains out."

"You could...but you won't."

"I could kill your right now."

"You're not gonna do that, either," he said, grasping my chin with one hand and planting a kiss on my lips. "Every night, King. I want your scent on my sheets, I want your body against mine, and I want that pussy on demand. Come home."

I hated when he touched me, when any part of his skin met mine. It was like there was a potion in his pores that made it hard for me to think. His touch, so fucking familiar, was like acid to my resolve.

"Fine. Will you go now?"

"I don't get to meet the fam, baby?"

"Hell the-fuck no!"

He grinned and was leaning in to kiss me again when a voice broke us apart.

"The hell you out here kissing a man like you sneaking or something for? Bring yo' mean self back in here so I can meet the man who got enough nerve to date you," my father yelled from the front door.

Shit.

. . .

Bo

HER FAMILY WAS...ECLECTIC. They were nice people, nicer than what I imagined she'd come from. Not that my love was evil, she was just not...nice.

"Well, Memphis. You gon' introduce your fellow?" her father boomed. The older man was big but smaller than I'd seen in past photos. He looked good for a septuagenarian.

Looking up from her plate at the huge table, Memphis said, "Oh, yeah...everybody, this is Mephibosheth Pierce. Mephibosheth, this is my family—my sisters, dad, stepmom or...moms?"

Oh, she was playing dirty as hell giving them my actual name.

Okay.

Bet.

The patriarch nodded. "That's right, my Candy is back from seeing the world!"

The ladies at the table gushed all over each other while Ray Nation's glare was nailed to me. I was sure he recognized my voice, but what was his issue? Considering the amount of money he made while working for me, he should've been elated to see me. Unless Memphis told him...

"Me and Denita are glad to have her back!" Mr. King said.

"I know I am. Frankie is too much for one woman. I need help," the wife, Denita, declared.

Well, damn. The old man had it like that?

"I'm happy to be home! I was sad to hear about Pauline, though. That was just...crazy," Candy, the returned wife, chimed in.

"Sho' was. Now, Metizodeck—" the old man began.

I decided to save him by saying, "You can just call me Bo."

"Yeah, I'll do that. What kind of name is Muhsleezoset anyway? Where your folks from?" her father asked.

"Uh, it's Biblical. I'm named after the grandson of King Saul," I informed him.

"The Bible. Now, that's some irony for you," Memphis mumbled.

"And I'm from Chicago. Still got folks there," I offered, ignoring Memphis because I had something for her ass later on.

"You don't say? I played a lot of shows in Chi," Frankie King replied, obviously having not heard his daughter's little remark.

"Oh, I know. My mom is a big fan of yours."

"Well, I hope to make her acquaintance one day. So...how did you two meet? You got to be something special because Memphis ain't brought a boyfriend around the family since high school."

"She hasn't?" I damn near squeaked.

"Hell naw, but I can usually tell when she got a man. She has a glow about her. Ain't seen it in a while, though. So, y'all must be just starting out."

"Actually—" I began, but Memphis cut me off.

She groaned, "Daddy, please! I'm almost fifty years old and Mephibosheth is older than me! We're both too grown for this level of interrogation. Besides, isn't this supposed to be a celebration? Candy's home and I'm happy about that. Now, Umber...what you put in this spaghetti? It tastes different, really good, though."

"Oh!" her youngest sister piped. "Deer meat."

"Uh, come again?" Memphis said.

"Deer meat. *Venison.* I killed a doe out by my house, skinned and dressed it myself and everything!"

There was a chorus of reactive groans from my table mates, and I just shrugged because the shit was good as hell.

Memphis

I WAS FUMING as I followed the piece of shit to his house. It didn't help that my entire damn family kept calling me back-to-back the entire drive. Of course, I didn't answer anyone. Not yet, anyway. I had to come up with a believable lie first because I damn sure wasn't telling them the truth. Hell, I *couldn't* tell them the truth, not even Lilith, who knew too much as it was. Ray obviously recognized Bo and knew the Cliff Notes version of our history and present arrangement, but he didn't know the true extent of the agreement I made with Bo in exchange for Lilith's life. He didn't know the gory details. He didn't know about the parts of the agreement I'd been successfully dodging for two years. Now, Bo was calling my bluff, and I most definitely wasn't ready to answer.

I trailed him to a modest neighborhood with virtually identical mid-sized homes, neat lawns, fenced in backyards, and HOA fees. Yes, the head of The Agency, an elite murder-for-hire firm, lived in suburbia, drove a damn Equinox, and usually wore a uniform of blue jeans and t-shirts. His immediate neighbors and The Village at large had no idea a billionaire was in their midst. If anyone asked, he told them he worked from home for a tech company—a shell company he happened to own.

I followed him into his driveway and then the garage, parking my car beside his. I kept my eyes on the spotless garage wall before me but could see him exit his vehicle and make his way to mine in my periphery.

When he tapped on my window, I rolled my eyes before lowering it.

"So, we calling in markers now? That's how you treat your 'love'?" I spat.

"Get out the car, King," he said, pressing a button on a fob.

As the garage door began to close, I felt like I was going to suffocate. I was really trapped on this man's property. This all felt too real. So, I said, "I don't want to be here."

Placing his hand on top of my car, he countered with, "And I *do* want you to be here."

I turned to look at him. "I don't care."

He shrugged. "That's fine. Now, get out the fucking car. If you're trying to start an argument, you ain't gonna win. You agreed to this shit."

"Under duress. Someone was trying to kill my sister!"

"And now no one can or will touch her."

I sighed, snatching the door open and hitting him with it.

He chuckled. "Violence will get you everywhere with me, baby. You know that."

I literally stomped inside his very neat and clean home, ignoring the shoe bench in the mud room because I knew he was anal about his floors being clean. No shoes allowed.

I didn't get too far before he grabbed my arm—this nigga was always grabbing me like I wasn't a fucking professional killer—and pulled me back to the bench.

"Fuck your floors. I ain't taking my damn shoes off until I'm good and ready," I shot at him.

He released my arm, grabbing the fabric of my nice red jumpsuit at the chest and pulling me into him. Then he kissed me long and hard, his hands cradling my face and moving to the straps of my jumpsuit, pulling them down my arms. In a literal second, I was naked, except for my shoes and bent over that bench...waiting, my legs rubbery and my heart pounding as I heard him unzip his pants behind me. By the time I felt his hands on my waist, I was trembling, and when he slid inside me, I dropped my head and whimpered.

"You're always so wet for me, so ready, but you keep fighting this shit," he groaned.

I couldn't respond. I honestly was having trouble forming coherent thoughts at that point because nothing, and I mean *nothing in the world*, compared to the feeling of this man inside me. Nothing ever had, and I was two thousand percent certain nothing ever would.

"You took this pussy away from me once. I won't let you do it again. Not...ever," he grunted, sliding in and out of me at the perfect pace—nice and easy and languid, which was actually torturous for someone like me. I liked frenetic sex because it felt unemotional to me. This? This relaxed, soaking sex? This felt too personal, and it scared me.

He was doing this shit on purpose.

"I took my body back. You didn't fucking deserve it!" I wailed. Damn, he felt impossibly, achingly divine.

"Nah, you ain't gon' make me go beast mode on you this time, no matter what you say. I'ma enjoy every ridge, every soft fold, and when I'm done, I'ma eat this motherfucker like it's the first meal I've had in years. Then, I'ma fuck you again and again and again, because whether I deserve your body or not, it's mine."

The thing was, he did not lie. He damn near fucked and ate me into oblivion and delirium that night.

5

"**W**hat the hell is going on?!" he yelled while standing in my front doorway.

"This is a quiet neighborhood, nigga. Pipe down," I replied.

"Then let me in!" He was actually getting louder.

"Can't do that. What you need?"

Zaccai's eyes narrowed at me. "I know the-fuck that woman is not here."

"I know the-fuck you ain't speaking on my woman. That's what *I* know."

"Moody told me you dropped your security last night, and I figured she had something to do with it. Pussy that good?"

"Come in, little brother," I offered, keeping my voice steady.

He smirked, stepping into the foyer. I closed the door and stared at my sibling for a moment before I spoke. "What were you saying?"

"I was asking if the pussy was that good. First, you pine over her for fucking decades. Now, you risk your life for her, worrying our mother and shit? She's a damn employee!"

Maybe I shouldn't have done what I did next, but he was talking about my woman, the love of my damn life. Brother or not, he'd crossed the fucking line. So, I lifted the gun I'd been holding, aiming it at his head. Side note: I never answered the door empty handed.

"You're gonna shoot your own fucking brother over some ass?!" he shrieked.

"*That* ass? Absolutely. Call my bluff. Say that shit again."

"You would break our mother's heart over a woman? Come on, Bo!"

I shrugged. "It is what it is."

When I looked up and saw Memphis at the top of the stairs wrapped in a sheet with her gun drawn, I smiled, and my heart started doing some of that Olympic breakdancing.

"I heard arguing. Would've come sooner but I had to piss," she explained, dropping her gun hand. She kept that shit on her, too.

My soulmate.

Zaccai turned to look at her, mumbling, "Damn, I forgot how fine she is."

"Nigga, I promise I will kill you," I gritted.

"Oh, it's him. I'm going back to bed," Memphis said, rolling her eyes.

Both me and Zaccai watched her leave because Memphis had an ass that could make a man change religions.

Then he said, "Pussy got to be top fucking tier with a body like that. She thick as a ham hock!"

So, I shot him in the right foot, or maybe it was the ankle. Either way, I shot his ass.

He howled as he fell to the floor.

"Stop all that yelling and shit. You know I got neighbors! Why you think I used a silencer?"

"Motherfucker, you shot me!" he wailed.

"Just a warning shot. Watch what you say about my woman. Now, get your ass out of here, bleeding all over my damn floor and shit."

"Nigga, how?! You shot me in my foot!"

"Crawl, slither, I don't give a fuck! Just go! And go out through the garage."

His dumb ass actually crawled out of my house.

ON DAY two of my captivity, I was fed, watered, and fucked relentlessly. At the present moment, Bo was devouring my pussy while I was bent over the bathroom vanity.

When he spread my ass cheeks and dragged his tongue up my crack, I cried out, "You so fucking nasty!"

Moments later, we were in the shower together, and I couldn't help thinking that maybe if he wasn't himself, this could be good. However, he *was* himself. He was vindictive and manipulative and heinous. He shot his own damn brother. He might've had a silencer on that gun, but I heard Zaccai hit the floor and howl. Plus, I saw Bo cleaning up the blood. He had the whole house smelling like bleach. I didn't bother to ask Bo why he did it because it didn't matter. What mattered was he shot his blood kin.

As he washed my body, I thought about how much I hated him... and how much I always would.

6

Memphis

"I've been calling you for fucking days! Why did you bring that man around my family?!" Ray thundered into the phone. I'd turned it off the night I arrived at my new prison and had barely powered it on the morning of day three of my captivity when his call came through.

"I didn't bring his ass. He followed me or had me followed or something," I informed him.

"So...you still messing with him?!"

"Is your wife still alive?"

Silence.

"Look, it is what it is. I can deal with it. He's..." I was going to lie and say he wasn't that bad. I mean, the dick was good, but to say he was tolerable was not factual. So, I settled on, "I'm fine with it."

"Memphis, you know I can't stand you, but damn. I don't like that you're tied to him."

I scoffed, "And you think I do? Look, he just wants to possess me. He won't hurt me. He...he thinks he loves me."

"He told you that?"

"When we were younger, he did." I omitted that my silly ass had reciprocated back then.

Fucking Pollyanna.

"Mem—" he began, but I cut in.

"I'll be fine, Ray. Just take care of my sister and nieces."

"Oh, I'ma always do that. I'm also gonna figure out how to get you out of this. Seeing him was fucking unnerving. He gon' be around the family all the time?"

"Nah. He really doesn't like people. Look, I need to call the rest of the fam." I mentally added, *while this asshole is gone for whatever business he's attending to.*

"Yeah, they all worried about you. They don't know how evil you are."

"Man, fuck you."

Then...

My mother's death affected me in many ways, the most profound being the toll it took on my sense of security. As a child, one never thinks about losing a parent, or at least I didn't because mine were always there when I needed them, especially my mother. She loved her babies to the ground, would do anything for us. While Daddy was out on the road, she happily stayed home with us even though she adored being with Fat Frankie King. She was beautiful, a beacon of light, and absolutely my champion. My mother was an angel whose absence left my world desolate.

So, after taking a year off from school to be with her, and after her death, to mourn her, I returned to college as a super senior. To further fill my time and occupy my mind, my twenty-two-year-old self picked up extracurriculars and hobbies like I was collecting Infinity Stones while diving headfirst into my studies.

I considered taking a Taekwondo class on campus but heard about an unorthodox, off-campus self-defense course. It wasn't something that was advertised. As a matter of fact, I got wind of it by eavesdropping while in the cafeteria one day. These two dudes were discussing what they called a lethal self-defense class, one designed to end your attacker rather than merely injure or disarm them. I was intrigued. So, I kept listening until I heard the instructor's name. Ironically, it was the same person who taught the Taekwondo class. I reached out to him, and now I was at the location—a nearly abandoned strip mall near my school—mere moments away from joining his newest class.

It was foggy that night, the rain that'd been pummeling the city for days having ceased just as I entered the building. I'd been kicking ass since I was little because I was a chubby kid that some liked to try to bully. They soon found out I was the real bully in the equation. My skill level grew as I aged, but I believed a class like this was essential to the Criminal Justice degree I was pursuing, although I wasn't exactly sure what direction I would go in with said degree. Maybe I'd become a police officer or a P.I. I could also work in crime scene investigation. Either way, I needed to be able to protect myself from the worst of the worst with or without a gun.

I was a little early for this class but not early enough to be the first student to arrive. That honor went to an older man with smooth mahogany skin, a bald head, and wide, perceptive eyes. He was tall and fit in his gray sweatsuit.

Upon seeing me, he lifted his sparse eyebrows, the look in his eyes flipping to a more lecherous expression. Most often, us chubby girls go from objects of ridicule to objects of desire as we mature. I had titty and booty for days, but his ass wasn't getting a taste of either.

Because...ew.

"You're new. I'm Lester," he said.

Lester the lecher, I thought, but in response, I said, "Nice to meet you. I'm Erica." Even back then, I didn't play that real name shit. "Erica Johnson."

"Pretty Erica. Nice to have some new blood in the class. I've been coming here for years."

"Years? Is it that difficult to master?"

He laughed. "Nah, just ain't got nothing better to do."

That almost made me smile.

Almost.

Soon enough, the space began to fill, and I distanced myself from Lester's ass. He was popular with the others, though. Several of them approached him as soon as they arrived.

When it was time for the class to begin, Lester moved to the front and spoke to the class in a different voice. So, *he* was the instructor. He'd been faking the old creep accent before, now speaking in a booming baritone. I mean, he *was* old but less creepy than he let on. Since I'd contacted him via email, I didn't know how he looked, and his name was listed as BT Riley. Obviously, he knew I lied about my name, too.

Whatever.

"Welcome back to our veterans, and welcome aboard to our newcomers. For those of you who don't know, I'm Bar Riley, your instructor. Here at Cave Martial arts, we are all about cooperative learning. So, any novice who has questions about what I'm teaching can feel free to ask any of the veterans for help, not just me," he said.

So, he lied about his name, too. I was beginning to like him.

But just a little bit.

"What I teach is a very lethal combination of Brazilian Jiu Jitsu and military LINE combat," he continued. "At the end of this class, you will be able to defeat your opponent and cause grave bodily harm, but you will also know when that is necessary. Now, let's get to work!"

And work we did.

~

I WAS ALWAYS someone who was naturally vigilant, constantly aware of my surroundings. It didn't hurt that I also had freakishly acute hearing. So that night, a month into the self-defense classes, I knew I was being followed as I left the strip mall heading to my car. The footfalls were soft, as if the person was trying not to be perceived—or since I was the last student to leave, perhaps they believed I was someone who was unaware of their surroundings—but I heard them, felt their presence, and it didn't feel like it was Mr. Riley. I could sense this was a stranger, a stranger who was *trouble*.

Although my heart raced, I kept my steps steady and deliberate. I didn't glance over my shoulder or do anything else that would lead someone to believe I knew what was going on. Arriving at my little Nissan, I unlocked the door and had opened it when I felt a hand on my left shoulder accompanied by a voice.

I spun around, quickly cutting his "Excuse me" off with a shot to his eyes, or maybe just his eyeglasses, from my keychain pepper spray and a swift knee to his groin followed by a hard punch to his nose. He was young, medium brown skinned, and okay looking, wearing eyeglasses that now sat crooked on his face. As he lay on the ground moaning, I lifted my right foot to finish him by stomping his head but paused when he screeched, "Wait! Wait! I have a business proposition for you," while squinting up at me. I knew his eyes were hurting like a bitch. Those glasses hadn't protected a damn thing.

Good.

"I'm not fucking you!" I yelled.

He vigorously shook his head. "No! No! Not that. The way you fight? That's a lucrative skill."

At that statement, I lowered my foot to the ground and said, "Talk."

7

Now...

I stepped into my mother's living room, noted the bodies occupying the space, and shook my head. This was what I left my woman for? I instantly turned to head right back out the door because...fuck this.

"Bo! Come in here and sit down!" my mother boomed, her strong voice contrasting her frail appearance. She'd always been a tiny woman, standing less than five feet tall, with a huge presence.

I turned to face her. "You said this was a family business meeting."

Nodding, she confirmed, "It is."

"Nah, can't be. If so, *she* wouldn't be here," I countered, nodding toward the very pretty woman sitting beside her on the sofa.

"She lives here. She *is* family, son. She's your wife."

"Ex-wife. Heavy on the ex."

"You know she is still family and always will be. Now, sit down, son."

I squared my shoulders. "Nah, I'll stand."

My beautiful, cocoa skinned mother sighed as she crossed her legs and clasped her hands over her knees. "Stubborn as ever. Fine, have it your way. After your father died, I chose you to run The Agency—although Zaccai is the oldest—because you are methodical, calculated, and always business minded."

"I know," I said, irritated as all fuck to be standing in this room with my mother, Zaccai's tattle telling ass, and got damn Layla—my ex—when I had the love of my life waiting for me at my house. I had pussy to eat, and I was standing there listening to my mom tell me shit I already knew.

"Then why are you letting your emotions lead you?"

It was time for me to sigh. "Zaccai got a slick mouth. You know that. I had to lay out some tread for his ass."

"Over a bitch, though? Over some old pussy? I gotta have surgery on my foot! The bones are fucked up!" Zaccai interjected, sitting in a chair with crutches beside him and that foot all wrapped up. He was so damn dramatic.

With a grin, I asked him, "You think you safe here? You think I won't shoot your ass again? You must've forgot that I keep that shit on me to be calling my woman a bitch."

"You absolutely will not shed blood in my house, especially not family blood!" my mother scolded.

"Yeah, that nigga do bleed a lot. Messed my floor up bad," I noted.

"Fuck you!" Zaccai bit out.

"I'm bringing Memphis to the next meeting. She's family to me," I advised the room at large.

"Man, you done lost your fucking mind!" Zaccai shrieked.

"Indeed, he has," my mother agreed.

"So, she's finally paying attention to you again? Wow. What'd you do? Blackmail her or something?" Layla finally spoke up.

Fucking bitch.

"You know what? Y'all go on with this meeting. I got better shit to do, like running the company that pays all y'all's bills but understand this: Memphis is my woman. Any disrespect toward her will not be tolerated from anyone," I advised.

"She's old and she can't give you children. She doesn't even want you," Layla said.

"And I don't want you. Now what?" I posed, my eyebrows raised.

No response.

"And Layla, I'll shoot your ass, too. Keep your mouth off my woman," I warned.

The room was deathly silent as I left.

Memphis

I WAS on the phone lying to Umber when he made it home.

Home?

Shit.

"So, you met him in college? You two dated back then?" she was asking.

"Kind of. We were basically doing back then what we're doing now. Fucking. You know my motto," I explained.

"Yeah, I do know...you don't fuck with men unless you're fucking them."

"Ding-ding-ding!"

"But you're living with him? That's what he said, right?"

"He says a lot of shit." When he appeared in the bedroom doorway, I added, "Gotta go, Umber. I'll call you back."

"Ah, Mr. Salt and Pepper Beard must have arrived. Have fun fucking!" She ended the call before I could respond.

I stared at him, at the relieved look on his face, and wished I would just off his ass, but for some reason, I wouldn't.

Or...couldn't?

That thought sent a chill up my spine, and I actually shuddered.

"Cold?" he asked, sounding all concerned and shit.

"No," I replied. "I need to go to my place and pick some things up."

"Everything you need is here. There's a closet full of new clothes and shoes. The kitchen is stocked, and a generous supply of dick is on tap and available at all times."

I just stared at him.

"I'll have someone pack up your apartment and bring everything here," he said.

"Everything? Ain't enough room in this house," I pointed out.

"I'll buy a new one."

Seated in his king-sized bed, I fell against the headboard. "Bo, if I wanted to escape, I could've done that while you were gone. I just need to go to my place. Alone."

Moving from the door to my side of his bed, he gazed down at me, licking his lips. "I can't let you do that. I can go with you, though."

"Hell no!"

He reclined his neck, a frown on his face. "You got a nigga hidden in there or something?"

"Yeah," I said, my voice deadpan. "What you gon' do, bust in there and shoot him like you did Zaccai?"

"Nah, I only injured my brother. I'll off any nigga who touches you. Hey, you miss me while I was gone?"

"Fuck no!"

Grinning, he grabbed my jaw, bending down to press a kiss to my lips. Then, he fucked the shit out of me...again.

8

Memphis

Then...

"The job is *what*? I mean...huh?" I asked, my voice hushed. This was a mistake. Meeting this stranger whose ass I'd recently kicked at a nearly empty diner across town was a humongous mistake in and of itself, but now that I'd heard his crazy business proposition, it was crystal clear just how young and dumb I really was. I mean, it'd been a couple of days since he approached me in that parking lot when I accepted his invitation, and to think, I'd *actually shown up* at this meeting. I was beyond stupid.

"You're made for this work. I've been watching you in the self-defense class. You enjoy inflicting pain," this nameless stranger said. His eyes were hidden behind a pair of sunglasses. It was late at night. I wondered if his eyes were still fucked up.

I truly hoped so.

"No, I don't!" I hissed under my breath. "I just...I like being safe."

He smiled while shaking his head, and I thought that was an odd sight, a true dichotomy. "You do and it shows. There's a light in your eyes when you're fighting," he said.

"Wait a minute. How long have you been watching me? I've never seen you before."

"*The Agency* sees all."

"What the hell are you talking about? Look, this is a little too crazy for me."

He removed the shades and stared at me for a few moments before saying, "I'm going to give you some time to think about it, Miss King. When you are ready to move forward, let Mr. Riley know. He'll get in touch with me, and we'll start your training."

Of course, he knew my fucking real name.

He stood to leave, dropping money on the table for our sodas, the only thing we'd consumed during this meeting.

"Wait...what is your name, since you already know mine?"

"If you decide to move forward, I'll give it to you."

The way he said that made me wonder if he was referring to his name or his dick, and well, what the fuck?

He left, and as I sat there pondering the entire interaction, a realization hit me. Riley. He'd mentioned Mr. Riley as a contact.

Again...what the fuck?

I DIDN'T WAIT for the next self-defense class to confront Mr. Riley. I didn't even wait a full twenty-four hours. I headed over to the athletics building before my first class, hoping Mr. Riley would be in his office. He wasn't, but after seeing the office hours posted on his door, I decided to wait. He'd be there in an hour.

He was late, so I ended up missing my first class. I hated that, but I'd make up for it. I had an A in that class anyway. Two hours later, I watched from my position standing beside his door as he approached with his head down, his stride purposeful. My fucking blood boiled.

Upon lifting his head and noticing me, his steps faltered, his eyebrows lifting and surprise illuminating his eyes.

"Miss Johnson," he said, a key in his hand as he eyed me. "Were you waiting for me?"

I nodded. "Yep."

"Well, I would tell you to schedule a meeting, but you're not an on-campus student of mine."

In reply, I stared at him, hoping to convey that I wasn't about to play some dumb ass game with him. Evidently, he got the message as he unlocked the door and invited me inside the small space.

Dropping in the chair behind his desk and placing his backpack on the floor beside him, the fit older man nodded toward a chair sitting in a corner. "Have a seat."

"I'll pass," I said with venom in my voice.

"Okay. Would you mind closing the door?"

I did, spinning around with my trusty pepper spray in my hand and leaning across his desk, placing the canister mere inches from his face as I growled, "Who the fuck are you, and what are you trying to get me into?"

He blinked a few times. "He told me about the pepper spray, said you really fucked him up."

"Yeah, you want some?"

"Nah, it's a bitch teaching classes with fucked up eyes."

"Then talk!"

"Okay...I, uh...noticed your talent. You're lethal. You were lethal when you joined my class. You're smart and fast with an appearance that belies all of that."

I frowned. "What do you mean?"

He shrugged. "You're gorgeous. *Black* and gorgeous. That alone is the perfect cover in this line of work. Black men will see you and want to fuck you. So will white men. White women will find you interesting, but they won't see you as a threat of any kind, and black women? They'll notice you, but the last thing they'll see you as is a killer. In a word, Miss King—I mean, Johnson—you're perfect for this job, a job that is very lucrative. In a few short years, you'll be able to stockpile enough money to live the life of your dreams."

So, he knew my real name just like his buddy did.

I eyed him as my brain completed a puzzle. "You...you are a..." I lowered my voice to a whisper. "...hitman?"

He smiled. "Now, I can't tell you that."

"And I can't just kill someone!" I uttered.

"Really? No one? There's no one in the whole world you want dead?"

Well, there was one someone, but he deserved it.

I must've unconsciously said that out loud because he pointed out, "Then you *can* kill someone."

My brow wrinkled, exposing my confusion, or maybe I was conflicted? Whatever it was made me pocket my pepper spray and hurry out of his office.

9

Now...

Hostage log, day three:
    I lay in his bed in the thick darkness of night with his body wrapped around mine. His warm, rhythmic breaths caressed my back as he slept. His hard dick was poking me in the ass. He felt...good, but that was nothing new. He always felt good. I just didn't want him to.

When I attempted to move, he groaned softly and kissed my back, his voice groggy as he inquired, "Where you think you going?"

"To pee, fool. Damn!" I snapped.

"So, you just wake up with an attitude?"

"When I'm dealing with you? Hell yes."

He chuckled in that stupid-ass, sexy way he always did, making me roll my eyes and clench my thighs. I hated the erotic muscle memory my body had for this man.

After moving my hair and kissing my shoulder, he backed away from me and smacked my ass. "Hurry back."

Moments later, I'd emptied my bladder and was at the sink washing my hands when something hit me, a weird, unfamiliar sensation that settled over me. Trying to shake the feeling off, I dried my hands and had moved toward the door when the room began to spin. I stumbled into the closed door, sliding to the floor, silently begging the bathroom to stop moving around me.

"King! King, you all right in there?!" Bo's voice sounded hollow and distant to me as I sat there with my eyes tightly shut, my hands on my head in an attempt to steady it.

"Y-yeah, I'm fine!" I tried to shout but my voice sounded weak in my own ears.

"You don't sound right. Open the door," he demanded, his voice almost shrill.

"I'm fine! Shit! I'll be out in a minute. Go back to bed."

I heard him mumble something about my ass being mean, and then nothing else from him.

I sat there for about thirty minutes before I felt steady enough to stand, and when I opened the door, Bo was posted on the other side of it. His eyes surveyed me as he grasped my chin.

"What's going on, King? What's wrong?" His voice was so soft and tender that I almost mistook him for a human.

"You. *You're* what's wrong. You and your refusal to leave me the fuck alone," I snarled as I pushed past him, heading back to his bed.

∼

"I RECEIVED some new intel from The Agency. The client has shared that the target, Senator Murray, will be traveling to a vacation home in rural Mexico in two weeks. Looks like this is our best shot. The area is supposed to be damn near desolate," I advised.

"Wow. So, the closed southern border, anti-immigration senator owns property in Mexico? What a fucking hypocrite!" Montana boomed into my ear.

"Don't forget their ties to human trafficking. I'd put money on the spot in Mexico being connected to that. I'm glad you're taking care of this piece of shit," Jerryn said.

I nodded even though neither of them could see me through the phone. "Me, too. Jerryn, you know what I need from you."

"Yeah, I'll make sure this is doable logistically, find out if there are any booby traps, and figure out travel."

"Good. Looks like we got a plan. I'll be back in touch with you two," I said, ending the call and looking up to find Bo staring at me with this puppy dog look on his face.

With a frown, I barked, "What?!"

He blinked and grinned.

Ugh.

"You usually plan hits naked and in a man's bed?" he queried.

"You usually kidnap assassins?"

Smiling, he crawled from his seat on the foot of the massive bed to where I sat up against the headboard, his knees on either side of my thighs as he cradled my face in his hands and kissed me. His exposed, hard dick brushed against my stomach, and I fucking melted because there was honestly nothing better than him being inside me. There was nothing better than his lips on mine, his arms around me, his skin against mine. All of that always reminded me of the past—us when we were much younger, before he broke my fucking heart. I was so enamored with Bo Pierce back then. I used to feel safe with him. Now I felt weak, powerless, and beholden to unwanted desires.

As he dropped his lips to my neck, I closed my eyes and reclined my head against the headboard. I didn't try to resist. Hell, I *couldn't*.

Instead, I reached between us and stroked him, hearing his breath hitch when my hand made contact with the silken skin of his shaft. Bo was in his fifties, but I swear his dick hadn't aged in the nearly thirty years since I first made its acquaintance.

He lifted his head, his eyes meeting mine before dropping to watch me stroke him, his chest heaving. He'd never stopped wanting me. I knew that. I felt it, too, but my bully had backed away when I demanded it of him all those years ago. Little did I know he was just biding his time, waiting for a slightly ajar door or inadvertently opened window, an entry point, and it came in the form of a hit on my little sister, Lilith. I'd do anything for her or Umber, including *him*. So, there I was, my mouth on him now. Not forced, not coerced, but voluntary because not only did I love the feel of him, I also loved the taste of him. I loved having him in my mouth as he fell apart. I loved hearing the anguish in his moans. I loved having him at my complete mercy. I loved...him. There, I admitted it. I'd loved him since I was twenty-two years old. Now, I was forty-seven. This shit was hopeless. *I* was hopeless. I tried for damn near three decades to purge him from my heart. Tried and failed, but while I could admit my true feelings for him to myself, I'd never admit it to him. Not that he was unaware, but I knew the power I'd be handing him in the form of a verbal admission, and I housed just enough animosity for him inside me to deny him that power.

I loved him.

I hated him.

And as he melted in my mouth...I knew I *owned* him. In all his cruelty and evilness, he was a kitten in my hands.

Selah.

10

Memphis

Then...

I accepted the proposition and was now in training to become an elite assassin, or at least that was how my recruiter termed it. Said recruiter, the man who I "met" in that parking lot, finally shared his name, or rather, his code name with me—11C22. The name assigned to me was B329. It was official; I was becoming a damn killer, and as I learned the fundamentals of surveillance, target research, and stealth, I already knew I was going to use these newly acquired skills to complete a side quest in the form of one Dr. Sherman Stone.

"You only have two major concerns other than hitting your target: not getting caught in the act and covering your tracks afterward," my recruiter was saying. We were in a room in an extremely seedy hotel. He'd swept it for bugs of the technical kind, but I was more concerned about actual insects because this place sucked!

I nodded my understanding.

"You're excellent at hand-to-hand combat, but you're going to have to become proficient with firearms of all kinds. Unless the client requests otherwise, most of your eliminations will be accomplished with a gun. It's quicker and cleaner. You ever handled a gun before?"

I shrugged. "I've shot one before, if that's what you mean. It was my daddy's pistol."

"Okay, get a gun. I'll teach you what you need to know to be proficient at shooting. The boss wants you working in the next month, so your learning will be accelerated."

"The boss? Do I get to meet him...or her?" I asked.

He grinned, and I finally noticed how handsome he was. *Too* handsome.

"No one gets to meet the boss," he informed me.

"Not even you?"

"Oh, I have, but I'm *me*," he quipped, his grin deepening by the millisecond.

I rolled my eyes and tried to ignore the flutter in my stomach.

I failed.

Damn, was I crushing on the tall, lean, butterscotch-skinned recruiter?

BETWEEN MY CLASSES and assassin training, I didn't have time for much else. So, I stopped attending the self-defense classes. There were only so many hours in a day and I was tired. Tired as hell, but I was learning a lot from my recruiter and spending so much time with him that it felt like we were growing closer, becoming...friends? More than friends? I could tell he liked me. I could *feel* it, but he was a killer.

Bitch, ain't you training to be one, too?

That thought made me shake my head at myself.

He eyed me, biting his bottom lip before saying, "You okay?"

I nodded a little too hard. "Uh, yeah."

"Okay, so I gotta tell you...you are crazy good at shooting. Shit, I don't think there's anything else for me to teach you."

I was seated beside him on the hotel bed, and although the room —our regular meeting place—was disgusting, being that close to him made it hard for me to focus.

Still, I managed to smile and say, "Oh, so I've hit expert level?"

"Pretty much!" He smiled at me, his eyes dropping to my mouth before he looked away. "Uh, okay. So, I think you're more than ready for your first assignment."

My eyes ballooned. "Really? Already?" I'd only been training for two months.

"Yeah. Remember, the boss set a deadline. You met it."

"Right..."

"I'll help you do any required research on the target. Expect a message on the cellular phone I gave you in the next couple of days with instructions for retrieving the job info. You said you know how to use it, correct?"

My eyes were still wide as I said, "Yes, my dad got me one just like it before I left for college. I hardly use it, though."

"Right. Um...can I ask you something?" he questioned, his voice suddenly timid.

I nodded.

"Do you...you got a man?"

My heart jolted as I answered him. "Not right now."

The corner of his mouth lifted in a lopsided grin. "Good to know."

11

Now...

"I told you I don't need you. I'll holler at you when I do," I said, moving to close my front door.

Moody blocked the door with his huge ass foot. "I know. Your moms didn't get the memo, though. She sent me over here."

"Okay, report back that you came, and I told you to leave."

"C'mon, man. You gotta call her or something, let her know I followed orders. She ain't just gonna take my word for it."

"*I'm* your boss, not her."

He shrugged. "She's my boss's mother. She gon' always pull rank as far as I'm concerned."

"I should fire your ass."

Again, he shrugged. He knew his job was safe since he'd been working for the company since I was a kid. Still, my mother using him to try and micromanage my life pissed me off. I'd sacrificed a lot for the family and The Agency, but I wasn't sacrificing Memphis, and her trying to make me keep using security was a part of that. It wasn't just about my safety. It was about control, and she could hang that up. I honestly didn't understand why she was still trying that shit with me.

"Just... hold on a minute," I said, lifting the phone I held in one hand. My gun was in the other. Before I could place a call to my mother, one from Memphis came in. I'd let her leave the house to meet with her team, so I wasn't going to miss talking to her.

Turning my back to Moody, I answered it with, "What's up, King?"

"Why you whispering? Your wife over there or something?" she replied.

"Don't play with me," I grunted.

"I'm not playing with you. Did you not marry her?"

"Did I not divorce her?"

"That's what you say..."

"So, you don't believe me now? Wait, are you jealous of Layla?"

"Why in the fuck would I be jealous of her? I'm actually pissed you two broke up. I liked that she took your attention off me."

I chuckled bitterly. "Nobody could ever do that, and you know it."

"You make it sound like you're obsessed with me. That's unhealthy; you know that, right?"

"Might be unhealthy, but it's true, and ain't shit I can do about it."

"Whatever. I was just calling to see if you plan on feeding me tonight or if I need to grab something before I come...before I return."

I grinned. "You almost said 'come home,' didn't you?"

"Hell no," she said matter-of-factly.

"And don't I always feed you? I have a chef, remember? He's preparing dinner right now."

"What do your neighbors think about you having a chef? Aren't you supposed to be a regular, middle class incel?"

I had to laugh at that dig. "An incel? Really? I'll remember that when I see you tonight, and my neighbors don't fuck with me just like I don't fuck with them."

"I hope you're right about that. I don't need you getting raided while I'm there."

"You ain't got shit to worry about. Just...I'll see you later."

"Yeah."

When I turned to face Moody, he was staring at me with this stupid-ass look on his face.

"What? You gonna report this call to my mother like I ain't fifty-four fucking years old?"

He shook his head. I'd never seen this big man smile. Moody's seriousness was as characteristic of him as that old-ass Starter jacket he wore and that newsboy cap sitting atop his balding head, but I could've sworn his eyes were smiling.

"No, I was just thinking about how fast you aged after your pops died. I ain't talking about your face or nothing. You just always seemed to be carrying the weight of the whole damn world on your shoulders, but seeing you now that you got that pretty lady back in your life? Man, you seem younger. She's really your one, huh? Gotta be 'cause she's so fucking mean."

I frowned. "You been eying my woman? You said she was pretty."

"Calm down, hot head. Don't shoot me like you did Zaccai."

Damn, I actually had my gun pointing at him with no recollection of lifting it from my side. "Watch your fucking mouth, then. Watch them eyes, too."

"You can't be with a beautiful woman and think no one will notice her beauty," he said.

I glared at him.

"Anyway, as head of security, I have to insist that we resume protecting you."

"I don't want anyone in the house. Y'all gotta stay outside somewhere inconspicuous. That's the best I can do."

Moody nodded and left.

Instead of calling my mother, I sent her a text: *back off*.

Memphis

"You done talking to your man so we can get down to business?" Jerryn asked as I ended the call with Bo. I only checked in with him so he wouldn't start acting stupid thinking I wasn't coming back.

"Fuck you. What you got for me?" I replied, reclining on the sofa in my apartment. I'd missed my place.

"Skirting around the subject, huh? Look, I know you're doing this for your sister—"

"Then you should also know I don't want to discuss this arrangement," I cut him off.

"Come on, Raja...I'm just worried about you. I know he's the one person who can hurt you. You brought up his ex-wife. That shit still gets to you."

Did it bother me that the man who long ago pledged his devotion and undying love to me married a whole-ass other woman? Yes, but more than that, it was how it all happened that broke the younger version of me. I wasn't sure I'd ever get past it, and it was only one of the reasons I hated loving him.

"Doesn't matter. I'm doing what I have to do. I would think you'd understand that."

He sighed. "She's my wife. I love her."

"And Lilith is my sister. I love *her*."

"Fine, whatever."

"Yeah, so you wanna do what I pay you to do? Get Montana on the phone."

Minutes later, I was listening to the young genius chatter on about the good senator's tech, or lack thereof, outside a couple cell phones, laptops, and tablets.

"I checked Murray's financials. Found the foreign accounts. The Senator has ties to that family in the UK that's deep into trafficking," Montana was saying.

"Well, that confirms my research and the info from the client," I mused.

"I bet the client is someone on their staff instead of a family member this time. Just a feeling I have. Anyway, I can also confirm that Murray is currently alone at the house in Mexico. The much younger spouse and small kids—there's like a twenty-year age gap, which is unsettling—are here in the states visiting family. So, this should be easy. There's no staff at the house. No chef or housekeeper," Montana rambled. This girl was a talker. She was also brilliant and loved guessing who our clients were.

"Yeah, logistically, this job is almost *too* easy. That bothers the shit out of me," Jerryn cut in. "This feels like a setup."

I frowned. "Then make sure it's not."

Jerryn nodded, a sober look on his face. He was younger than me, but you couldn't tell by looking at him. He was something past light skinned as of late. He was pale and getting skinnier by the year. I wondered if it was the job or just life in general.

For me, it was both.

12

Memphis

I was dizzy again, so dizzy I couldn't make myself leave the parking lot of my apartment building, although I knew I needed to. I needed to get back to Bo's place before he tried to kill Jerryn or something, but the inside of my vehicle would not stop spinning. Hence, I rested my head on the steering wheel hoping that I'd feel good enough to drive soon. My forehead had just rested on the leather when a knock on my window startled the hell out of me.

My eyes popped open to see a frail figure standing next to my car in the waning sunlight.

Sighing, I lowered the window. "I'm not in the mood for you today, old lady."

Bo's hag of a mother smiled, displaying perfectly straight teeth that my labor probably paid for. "Oh, you know I don't care about your moods, honey. We need to talk. You seem to have a short memory."

"Go talk to your son. I'm just a mere employee. He's running the show."

"Memphis, you are well aware of the power you have, the *hold* you have, on my son."

"Mrs. Pierce, leave me the fuck alone."

As she began to speak, I started my car and drove my dizzy ass off the lot. I hoped I ran over her foot or something because I could not stand her.

Never could.

"YOU BETTER PUT your mother on a fucking leash! I didn't sign up to have to deal with her!" Memphis shrieked the moment she stepped in my house that night.

To be honest, she startled the shit out of me, and that wasn't easy to do. So, it took me a minute to reply, and that was a minute too long. As soon as I opened my mouth to speak, she continued her rant.

"You said things would be different. That was part of our agreement, too! You fucking promised I wouldn't have to see or talk to your mother and the bitch shows up at my place harassing me! I'ma shoot her ass next time!"

The fuck?

My mother had started fucking with Memphis now? It took everything in me not to go to her house right that moment, but I had to exercise some restraint. I had to calm my lady down. I had to make sure she was good. Nothing was more important than that, than *her*.

I abandoned the stool I was occupying and moved closer to where she stood in the doorway of my kitchen, placing my hand on her soft cheek. Of course, she swatted it away.

"Don't fucking touch me!" she growled, her full lips trembling. Her flawless brown skin was flushed, her round eyes narrowed. "You are enough to deal with! I can barely breathe around you. I'm dealing with all these mixed emotions and shit because you're an asshole—"

"An asshole who loves you," I cut in.

Before I could blink, her fist met my nose.

"Fuck!" I yelled, holding my damn nose. The motherfucker started bleeding.

"Don't you say that to me! I told you to never say that to me again and I meant that shit!"

"Got damn, King! I think you broke my nose! I *do* lov—"

My words stopped when she produced a gun, aiming it at my head. We were only inches apart, but the thing was, Memphis King wouldn't miss even if the length of a football field separated us.

At night.

With no lights.

During a fucking sandstorm.

"Say that shit again and I will gleefully end you! Fuck feelings or good dick or your family's retaliation. I'll kill them, too!" she advised me, no longer yelling. Her voice was calm and very collected.

She meant that shit.

"Memphis..." I began.

"King!"

I sighed, now tasting my own blood as it oozed from my nose into my mouth. "King, come here."

She backed further away from me and lifted her free hand, using it to steady the already stable gun. "Why?"

I decided to take a chance, inching forward and lifting my hand to push the gun aside as I eased closer to her, holding her face in my hands. Her lips quivered as she stared at me, her eyes telling me what I already knew, what I'd always known. She loved me. She loved me almost as much as I loved her, but I'd hurt her. My entire family hurt her. The Agency hardened her. Still, the eyes staring into mine at that moment didn't belong to the woman who held on to the hurt I caused all those years ago. They belonged to the twenty-something year-old who captured my heart and kept it under her control every day since. Her breathing was harsh as I lowered my bloody face to her immaculate one and kissed her, her soft body instantly melting into mine. My hands trembled like they always did when she let me touch her like this. My heart hammered, and I felt a little woozy—side effects of one Memphis Blue King.

First, I heard the gun fall; then I felt her arms loop my neck, and finally, she wrapped those thick thighs around me, making my dick virtually rip through the fabric of my pants. Confession: I'd never desired any woman the way I desired her. No other woman had come close to satisfying me like she did. No other woman took my breath away while simultaneously being the oxygen that kept me alive. The possibility of us one day reconciling was my only reason for climbing out of bed for nearly thirty years. Well, that and making money. I was fond of making money, too. But Memphis? She was it, my one and only.

I gripped her round ass, kissing her and moaning into her mouth, the taste of my blood combining with her minty freshness. I needed to be inside her like yesterday. Wait, I *was* inside her yesterday. Amendment: I needed to be inside her all day every damn day. So, I walked us to the kitchen island, knocking the stool I'd abandoned aside before sitting her on the granite surface. The only sound in the room was our breathing as we ended the kiss and went to work undressing, our movements hasty and uncoordinated and frantic. Hell, I didn't even bother to take my pants and underwear completely off, letting them pool around my ankles on the travertine floor. I didn't bother to take my shirt off at all. Who had time for that shit when the best pussy in the free world was sitting right in front of me, ready to receive me?

I stepped between her legs, grasping her thighs and pulling her to the edge of the island, my dick jumping and leaking with anticipation. I could smell her pussy, the scent driving me something several miles past wild. Feral was a weak word, too. Was there a word to describe how unhinged her pussy, her body, her *being* made me feel?

Hell. No.

I leaned in to kiss her, but she halted my progress with a hand to my chest. I can't lie; I was considering begging her to let me inside that pussy at that point, and if that didn't work, a death threat wasn't off the table.

I needed that crack between her legs...expeditiously.

Her long lashes fluttered as she moved her face closer to mine, so close that her breaths filled my nose. I closed my eyes and involuntarily moaned, expecting her to kiss me. Instead, she used that talented tongue of hers to clean my face, mopping up the still oozing blood with it. Something about the twistedness of that act sent my immoral ass over the proverbial edge. Somehow, I let her finish before grabbing the back of her head and kissing her so hard and deep that the shit was actually uncomfortable for me, but I didn't care and neither did she.

My fucking twin.

In quick succession, I was inside her while silently begging my knees not to buckle and my nuts not to prematurely empty. I didn't understand how every time with this woman felt as good as the first time. Nah, it felt better.

And better.

And fucking better.

I drove into her, backed up, and slammed forward again, her wails filling my ears as my heart felt like it could explode at any minute, and when her walls began to shudder around my dick, I whimpered, "I love you. I love you. I love you..."

And I did. Consequences be damned.

THE NEXT MORNING, I reluctantly left my bed and the woman who shared it. Stepped right past Moody, who was posted up in my garage, climbed into my car, and made the familiar thirty-minute drive from The Village to the Coventry Woods Estates subdivision situated on the other side of Parkton in a more rural area. Moody had followed me, trailing me through the gate after I entered the code and pulling into the driveway seconds after I did. I knew he'd be on my tail, and I didn't give a fuck. I had some shit to attend to.

I entered another code into the keypad by the front door, and despite the early hour, began yelling the names of the house's occupants. Standing in the huge foyer, I observed as one by one, they descended the stairs—my mother, Zaccai, Layla, and last but not least, a twenty-eight-year-old man who hated my guts.

My son.

The feeling was lowkey mutual, though.

It's a long story.

"What the fuck, man?! That bitch leave you or something? She the one who fucked your nose up?" Zaccai whined, his voice groggy and his face crusty.

I blew out a breath and shook my head. "You just never learn, do you?" I said, and then I shot him in the left leg—I liked symmetry— watching as he crumpled to the floor. "Next time, I'm hitting your ass above the fucking waist. Consider this your last warning!"

Everyone started yelling, and Moody actually reached for his gun, but I turned on him before he could grab it.

"What you gon' do? Shoot me? I pay your salary! Stand the-fuck down!" He kept that hand under his jacket, so I added, "Moody, I don't care about what you meant to my father or how many years of service you've given my family. Stand the-fuck down before I *put* you down!"

He raised his hands and backed up.

Keeping my eye on him, I lifted my gun, aiming at the foyer walls as I pulled the trigger over and over again, hitting paintings, light fixtures, any and everything. Layla was yelling, Zaccai was on the floor crying, my son was shooting daggers at me with his eyes, and my mother? She just stood there staring at me like the stone-cold bitch she was.

"Dear Mother, I don't know if you recall this, but we had a deal that included you steering clear of my lady. So, consider this my last time saying this to you... stay THE FUCK away from Memphis. Don't talk to her, don't talk about her. Hell, don't even *think* about her. I will fuck your entire world up for her and that goes for all of you, but especially you, Mother. You fucked us up once. You took her from me, but you won't do it again. I'll burn your whole world down before I let that happen! And you know I can do it!"

With that, I left.

13

Memphis

Then...

L ife could be so crazy.

In what felt like seconds, I went from being a regular-degular college student with a few insecurity and anger issues who was a bit of a loner but managed to be friendly with her dorm-mate and some of her classmates to being a trained assassin with a cute and kind of sexy recruiter-slash-mentor. Or rather, I was an assassin in training...I guess.

I mean, I'd always been good at kicking asses, but it turned out I wasn't too shabby at shooting asses, either. I practiced at a shooting range on the outskirts of town religiously. Used some of the money my father kept in my account to buy two guns—a twenty-two to start, per my mentor's instructions, and a Glock once my shooting skills improved.

The Glock was my favorite.

I used 10mm rounds since 11C22 said using them made the Glock most powerful. I practiced and practiced, garnering appreciation from the others—mostly men—I encountered at the range. So, that was my life...practice, school, and waiting. I waited...and waited...and waited some more—patiently at first—for that message from my recruiter. Weeks passed. Then months. I met 11C22 in the fall, and the spring semester ended without a word from him. I graduated and returned home to Parkton from Romey. Did my employers know that? Or maybe they changed their minds? Was I fired? If so, why? And well, shouldn't I have been happy about it? It was a good thing to know I wasn't going to be an assassin, risking my life and freedom to kill people...right?

Wrong.

Maybe I was evil or twisted or just plain insane, but the thought of not pursuing this new career upset the hell out of me. Perhaps it was the mindset I adopted in order to believe I could do it or the preparation or...the adrenaline, the rush I felt when I pulled a trigger, or when I was still taking the self-defense class, the jolt of serotonin that flooded me when I fucked someone up with a kick or a throat punch. Not to mention the fact that I would eventually be able to choose my targets. That way, I could do for others what I hadn't been able to do for myself and my family—get revenge, punish those for whom punishment was egregiously overdue. That's what it was. I could avenge my beautiful mother's death through these other people, and that had my mind all tangled up. It physically hurt that she was gone due to negligent care from her doctor, a misdiagnosis, and a broken system. Worse than experiencing her passing was witnessing the suffering she was forced to endure. That broke me, shattered my heart, and gave me literal PTSD. I wouldn't survive witnessing another loved one going through that.

I was pissed and incredibly angry because someone needed to pay for my loss, and I no longer had the possibility of a proxy.

"What's got your mean self frowning, girl? You pissed at the TV? It ain't even on." My father's voice startled me, and I realized I'd been glaring at the TV as I pondered my situation.

I smiled up at him as he stood over me. He'd always been a big teddy bear of a man. "Just thinking."

"Mm-hmm," he grunted, toddling out of the living room. "Don't think too hard. You look like you two shakes from cutting someone's whole head off."

I rolled my eyes. "I love you, too."

He stopped and turned to look at me, concern in his eyes. "You still going through with it?"

"I don't have any other choice."

Giving me a sober look, he nodded his understanding.

THE BIG DAY HAD ARRIVED, and I was nervous as hell. I'd fought hard to get to this point, and in the end, my father had to step in to make it happen, but now I was here. It was the right thing to do, and I knew it, but that didn't make it any less devastating. At the age of twenty-two, I was just minutes from having a hysterectomy as a means of prophylaxis. My sisters weren't as pragmatic as me, but then again, I'd always been the most analytical of the three of us. My decision wasn't made totally out of emotion. To me, it just made common, mathematical sense. My mother suffered and died from uterine cancer that, by the time it was definitively discovered and diagnosed, had ravaged her body, having spread to her pelvic lymph nodes, cervix, and vagina. She fought long and hard. I never wanted to go through that, so there I was. The having kids thing didn't move me. I would've rather been childless than leave children behind to mourn me while they were young. I wanted to live, see the world, maybe even fall in love. I had an uncertain future ahead of me, but I wanted time to figure it out.

I smiled as my father kissed my forehead and my sisters hugged me before they took me back for the procedure. I was ready to get this over with and move on with my life.

14

Memphis

Then...

I had too much time on my hands, or at least that was the excuse I came up with. During my recovery from a successful surgery, I had too much time to reminisce and ponder and stew in a bitterness I couldn't seem to shake. I also had new skills that I wanted —no—*needed* to utilize: research and elimination. However, I had no mentor, no company to work for, and no clients. I had no idea how to get in touch with The Agency or 11C22 himself. I tried calling the number he gave me, but he never answered, and the burner I kept charged and ready never rang. Were there other companies of the like that I could apply to? Did that even make sense?

I was frustrated and restless, and that was why I was sitting in my car after ten in the evening, using the high-tech binoculars I'd bought for my "job", waiting to see Dr. Sherman Stone leave his office for the third night in a row. He usually made his departure around six or seven in the evening. Most days, he left the home he shared with his live-in girlfriend around 5:00AM and headed to the gym. Afterwards, he returned home and emerged an hour or so later to head to the hospital or his office.

I watched him leave the building, walk to his car, and open his car door, retrieving something before heading back into the mile-high structure in midtown Parkton. I'd watched the staff and the last patient leave earlier. He was alone, but for how long, I wasn't sure. I also didn't care. This was my best chance to get it done, so I took it.

I left my car, walking in the darkness through the three parking lots that separated me from the doctor, all the while thinking about how my mother described her symptoms and fear to him and how he dismissed her, saying she was being dramatic and that it was probably just a fluctuation in her hormones. She begged this man to help her to no avail. She trusted him to the point that my father had to damn near order her to seek a second opinion, and Kola King didn't take orders from nobody, not even the love of her life.

I stepped into the St. Raphael Medical Tower wearing all black with padding on my body to make me appear bigger and lifts in my shoes to belie my height, as my mentor had taught me to do. Hell, I even did my best impression of a man's gait and had used a binder on my breasts. Navigating my way through the building, I made the journey to my destination while avoiding the surveillance cameras I'd taken note of when I paid the building a visit shortly after I returned home from college.

Yeah, I'd been planning this for a long time.

A crazy long time.

The door to Stone Women's Clinic was unlocked, but if it hadn't been, I would've picked it. That was another skill I'd taught myself. With my gloved hand gripping my Glock, I stepped through the dark office toward the only light in the space. Jazz was playing, and when I finally reached the source of the sound, I found the doctor's personal office empty. Bathroom break, maybe? A flushing sound coming from a door to my left told me I was correct. So, he had his own little restroom? Well, that was nice.

When he emerged from the lavatory wiping his hands on a brown paper towel, I smiled and lifted the gun. The movement made his eyes snap up to me, and I could see disgust quickly shadow his face. Dr. Stone was a handsome, older Black man with midnight skin who, according to his posts in a private online group for doctors I'd infiltrated, hated Black women. He was sick of them and wished he didn't have to see them as patients, an attitude that most certainly influenced the level of care he provided to said women.

Misogynoir at its finest.

Not to mention that the nigga killed my mother, or at least that was how I saw it, and my opinion was the only one that mattered in this instance. So, before he could move a muscle, including his tongue, I shot him dead between his fucking eyes.

The following evening, I finally received a message to my burner phone that read: *2:00 PM tomorrow at Miss Katie's Katfish Kitchen. Ask for Donnie.*

15

Now…

She always smelled so good, fresh, even after spending hours beneath me or on top of me. Her sweat, her pheromones, her pussy—it all bore an intoxicating fragrance that I was addicted to. I'd always been addicted to it.

At that moment, we lay facing each other, my mouth buried

between her breasts which were moist with perspiration, a combination of both mine and hers.

"You're fifty-four years old. How the fuck do you have this much stamina to be having all this sex?" she murmured.

I chuckled, kissing her cleavage. "I been saving all this energy for you," I admitted.

"You act like you've been celibate or something," she scoffed.

"You assume I haven't?" I said against the soft skin of her breasts.

"I *know* you haven't. You have an entire wife."

I lifted my head, just barely able to discern the features of her face in the near blackness of our bedroom. Our bedroom, our house. Everything I owned and was belonged to her, too, whether she wanted it that way or not.

"*Had.* Stop tryna give that woman to me, King."

"No, your father gave her to you. I'm clear on that."

I sighed, moving up in the bed until my face was even with hers. "All I've ever wanted was you. You know that." I pulled her body into mine although she was now far less pliable. She was pissed; our past had a way of ruining her mood.

"Bo—"

"I love you. I know it makes you angry for me to say that, but it's the truth, and you know it. You *feel* it. Was I fucked up in the past? Yes. Am I even more fucked up now? Yes. But all that I do or have done, however twisted it may be, is a side effect of being without you for far too long. I need you."

"Shut up," she grated.

"King—"

"I said, SHUT UP!" Her voice was so loud as she literally yelled in my face that I actually flinched.

And I never flinched.

She shoved me onto my back, and before I could blink, her hand was on me, stroking me, and like a bell's toll to Pavlov's dogs, my dick sprang to attention.

All I could do was close my eyes and murmur, "Shit..."

Her mouth met my left nipple, her teeth digging into it as she continued to stroke me. The nipple shit hurt, but I liked it, and she knew it. There wasn't another woman in the world who knew my body like Memphis King did.

She moved, abandoning my dick to straddle me, replacing her mouth on my chest with her pussy, and I could smell it, damn near taste it.

Got damn, I wanted to lick it!

"I gave you my heart when I was young, and you broke it like it was nothing. I loved you so much," she said as she rubbed her pussy on my chest.

Reaching up, I grasped her hips. She was going to make me lose my fucking mind. "I've said it before and I'll say it again...I'm sorry, baby. I fucked my own heart up in the process, too. Hurting you destroyed me."

"Destroyed you? Destroyed *you*?" she said, her voice breaking, and before I could elaborate, offer a rebuttal, take a deep breath, *anything*, she slid that pussy over my chin, taking a seat on my mouth and making me moan from somewhere deep in my soul as I went to work, licking and sucking her clit. She gripped my head and rode my tongue with abandon, devoid of any regard for my need of oxygen. Her thick thighs flanked my face as she grinded and bucked and howled. I just kept feasting on her flesh like my life depended on it. Hell, maybe it did. When that orgasm hit her, she tried to run away, but I reached up and gripped her ass cheeks, holding her in place, and when I knew she couldn't take anymore, I released her, allowing her to collapse onto the bed beside me.

As I fought to catch my breath and listened to her do the same, I managed to say, "You can hate me. I don't care as long as I get to love you. That's all I want. I just want to love you."

Her response was to leave the bed and shut herself in the en-suite bathroom.

Memphis

Now...

"YOU'VE BEEN AVOIDING ME," Lilith accused.

"No," I replied, my voice modulating on the "o."

"Yes," she countered, mimicking my tone.

I sighed, reclining on her sofa. "Ask your questions, Lil."

"Okay, who was that man with the Darth Vader energy that came to Daddy's house?"

"Who, Ray? Isn't he your husband?" I asked, my eyebrows knitted together.

She glanced at her daughters playing on the living room floor. They were so cute, but I was sure they had kid cooties.

"Bitch, you know I'm not talking about the man I freshly fucked this morning," she harshly whispered. "You know who I'm talking about!"

"Um, ew?" I said, holding my stomach.

"Memphis, come on!" she whined. "Who is he?"

I sighed. "He's the reason you're still alive." Fuck it. I was tired of lying to her.

She frowned. "What? What do you mean?"

"He's my boss, among other things. He, uh...canceled the hit on you."

"Your boss? You're fucking your boss?! You're living with him?!

Wait, I would've thought he'd be taller than that. Big, menacing. You know?"

"You met him. Do you think more height would make him any more threatening? You just said he has Darth Vader energy."

"Oh, you're right. If he was bigger, I'd probably would've cried when I met him."

"Exactly."

"Then why in the world are you with him?"

"I just told you why. He saved your life."

"Wait, so you're...oh. Memphis. I'm sorry. I don't want you to have to trade yourself for me."

I leaned forward, fixing my eyes on the coffee table. "That's not the only reason I'm with him. You remember how we talked about men like Ray and how they're addictive? You asked me about my Ray. This is him."

"Ohhhhh!" She was so loud with that one word that Blaze glared up at us...with her little mean self. Dropping her voice, Lilith added, "But didn't you say he wasn't kind to you? He's not hurting you, is he?"

"You think I'd let him?"

"Right, that was a stupid question."

"Uh-huh. Look, it's complicated. *Really* complicated, but it's whatever. I'm fine. He thinks he loves me."

"And you love him," she stated. It wasn't a question but more of a revelation.

I couldn't respond.

"GET DRESSED. We're going to dinner, so put on something nice." Bo's voice entered the living room before he did, booming in that way that always made me tingle down below.

I hated that feeling.

"What? You fired the chef whose name I'm not allowed to know?" I said without bothering to look up from my phone.

He'd entered the room and was standing over me now. "Call him Chef, like I already told you to. My name is the only one I wanna here you say in this house."

I shifted on the sofa, looking up at him. Same old evil ass, hand-some ass Bo. Glasses in place, beard and hair neat. I involuntarily smiled. "Fresh cut?"

He moved, squatting in front of me, his hand on my knee. "Can't walk around looking crusty with you on my arm now, can I?"

I rolled my eyes.

He grinned, rubbing his beard. "*And*, I had to get your seat right."

Skipping over that statement, I asked, "Where are we going?"

"It's a surprise. Hurry. We're gonna be late," he ordered before standing and leaving the room.

THIS WOMAN LOOKED SO FUCKING good; I wasn't sure what the fuck to do with myself. It was one thing to spend time with the love of my life, but to see her in this black dress that looked like it was made just for her body? That red lipstick? That fucking perfume? I was about to pull my car over and eat every morsel of her pussy.

Shit!

"You look good, King. Maybe a little *too* good. Got me wanting to lock you up and throw away the key," I said, reaching over to lay a hand on her thigh.

She swatted it away. "You're already holding me hostage, remember?"

"Yeah, but I think you kinda like it. I know you like how I make you feel, huh?"

"Where are we going?"

"You'll see, beautiful."

She mumbled something I couldn't make out, and I smiled. She hated being in the dark about things as much as I did. Side effects of the job.

When we arrived at our destination, she shifted her body, facing me with a frown. "Why are we at The Greenwood? Damn, why is the parking lot full?"

"It's a birthday party. Let me open your door for you, baby."

"Don't start that *baby* shit," she fussed. "And who the hell would invite your evil ass to a birthday party?"

"I have friends, King. People like me."

"Impossible."

"You nervous or something?"

Her eyes narrowed. "Hell no! Why would *I* be nervous?"

"I don't know. Maybe you think one of your other niggas might be in there, and of course, in that case, I'ma have to kill them."

"Did I kill your wife?"

"I didn't expect you to. I'm the only one of the two of us who's in love...right?"

"Correct, but maybe I would kill her just to hurt you," she posed, her right eyebrow arched.

"Now, you know that wouldn't hurt me. Someone wants to mess my head up, let them touch *you*. I'll fuck everything and anything up over you."

She chuckled bitterly. "Riiiight...you gonna get the door or what?"

I climbed out the vehicle, noting Moody's car parked behind mine as I walked around to her door.

Memphis

HE GUIDED me into the building, his hand on the small of my back, his body heat and scent making me more than a little woozy. The history between us made being with him both nostalgic and heart-breaking. He was my first love, and the worst thing about that was he knew it.

As we were greeted by the hostess, who was eyeing him like he was a brand-new Birkin, he let his hand drop to my waist, pulling my body into his.

"Pierce," he said, his voice as commanding as ever.

The hostess dropped her gaze to a bundle of papers that lay on the podium before her, quickly jerking her head back up. With wide eyes, she said, "Yes, Mr. Pierce! So good to have you with us tonight. Let me show you to your table."

Bo grasped my hand as we followed her into the massive space teeming with elegantly dressed brown bodies. Several people greeted Bo as we threaded our way through the maze of round tables to our own. Others may not have spoken to him, but their eyes were on him. They had to feel it, that pull he had, that invisible but absolutely undeniable magnetism that allowed him to own any room he entered.

Once we were seated, I fixed my eyes on him.

When he finally looked at me, he smiled. "I'm known for giving great gifts."

I shifted my gaze to our surroundings and smirked, knowing that wasn't the truth. The truth was he oozed power and anyone with a pulse could feel it. "Oh, really? That's it?" I questioned.

Leaning in close to my ear, he murmured, "Nah, it's you. They've never seen a woman so beautiful, so fucking fine. They want you, baby."

I turned my head, frowning as he stared at me. "Everybody, Bo? They *all* want me?"

He nodded, licking his lips. "All of them. I hope I don't have to kill anyone tonight."

Shaking my head, I said, "There you go, tryna act like this thing between us is real."

With a peaked eyebrow, he replied, "This thing between us is *extremely* real to me. I love you. I have loved you from afar for damn near three decades. I dreamed of being with you again. If I had one goal in my life, it was you. You're everything to me, King."

There was sincerity in his eyes and his voice, but I couldn't let myself accept his words. That would be dangerous.

"Stop," I hissed. "I'm willing to play this little game with you for the sake of my sister, but we're not going to pretend this is some star-crossed lovers shit. You didn't choose me when you should've. Nothing will change that."

He had the nerve to look hurt, so I gritted, "Fix your damn face."

His eyes flashed before he grasped my chin, pulling my face so close to his that his lips touched mine as he spoke.

"You don't get to tell me how I feel. You don't get to rewrite history. I love you whether you fucking like it or not. This shit between us is real, whether you like it or not, and I've always, *always* chosen you... whether you believe it or not." His voice was a low growl.

Oh, so I'd pissed him off, huh?

"Fuck. You," I rebutted, my words slow and deliberate. "Fuck you and your declarations and lies and bullshit."

Before he could respond, a voice said, "Rochelle? I thought that was you! Been a long time!"

I almost asked the tall, light skinned man standing before us who the fuck Rochelle was, but then I realized he was someone I once knew and fucked. Of course, he didn't know my real name.

"Uh, hi...um..." I muttered.

"George...George Carson."

"Yes, George! Crazy seeing you here!"

"Right!"

Cue awkward silence until...

"I'm Bo, George."

I didn't have to look at my boss, the dicktician, to know he was tight. If the energy he was now giving off didn't tell me, his voice did. Still, I gave him my attention and watched as he stood, moving around the table to offer a hand to George. A smiling George took it, and Bo yanked him forward, saying something in his ear before shoving him away. George left rather swiftly without another word to me.

"The fuck did you say to him?" I asked once Darth Maul reclaimed his seat beside me.

Settling in his chair, he shared, "I told him if he ever came around you tryna get a whiff of your pussy again, I will gladly dislocate his dick and both his balls after I cut his head off."

"Now, why would you say that to him? George is a good guy, and if I remember correctly, he had some good dick, too."

He glowered at me, his nostrils flaring. "Keep fucking playing with me and you will become a prisoner for real. You better hope no other niggas approach you tonight because I'll fuck this whole building up."

"You gonna fuck me up, too? You think I'd let you? And as far as me being a real prisoner, I'll kill you first."

He leaned in, kissing me before I knew what was happening. When our lips parted, he said, "I don't doubt you will, and you might have to if you think I'll ever let you go otherwise."

The night's MC kept me from responding, as the festivities began.

IMAGINE my surprise when I discovered this was the mayor's birthday party. The mayor of Parkton, that is, who was now making a bid for a US Congress seat. What the fuck were we doing at Mayor Shari Young's birthday party? The question played in my head as we ate the too-good soul food dinner and sat through the speeches from her friends and colleagues, but as soon as the DJ started playing music and the dance floor began to fill, I turned to him, ready to get an answer to my burning question.

But then I heard, "Mr. Pierce, so glad you could make it tonight."

It was the got damn mayor!

The fuck?

Bo stood to greet her with a quick hug and a peck to her cheek. "Where else would I be, Mayor? You know I had to come celebrate with you."

"Well, I appreciate you, as always, and thank you for the gift." Damn, her scrawny ass was gushing all over this nigga.

The hell?

"You're welcome! And this lovely lady is Memphis King. She's a local business owner."

"Oh! Really?" she squeaked, her overly enthusiastic attention now on me. "So good to meet you! What's the name of your business?"

She'd moved closer to my side of the table, her hand outstretched.

I took it and gave her a fake smile. "Likewise. I own a day spa— Face Card. It's over in the Montblanc shopping center."

Her mouth fell open. "What?! That's where I get my facials! That place is fabulous! Why have I never seen you there?"

I shrugged. "I'm a hands-off business owner. My staff is more than capable of keeping things afloat."

"Oh, I agree! Wow, Mr. Pierce, you've got yourself quite a catch!"

Bo smirked. "Believe me, I know I do."

The mayor left after the two shared another hug, and he grasped my hand.

"Dance with me, King," he said, and as much as I wanted to refuse, I couldn't. After all, he was touching me.

So I stood, allowing him to guide me to a spot on the dance floor situated in front of the stage and pull me into his arms as Lucky Daye's *Diamonds in Teal* played. It was a beautiful song, one of my favorites, really, and despite it all, he felt good...as always.

Leaning in close to his ear as we swayed to the music, I said, "You fucked the mayor," rather than asking the question. It was too damn obvious. "I know you have a *negro's only* dick, so I can see it since she's Black, but she's a bit thin for your taste, don't you think?"

He turned to face me, his eyes smiling. "You jealous?"

"She wants some more, too. It's written all over her," I said, ignoring his dumb ass question.

"Like it's written all over you, right?"

I rolled my eyes.

He grinned. "Don't worry, she ain't got nothing on you."

"Shut up and dance, nigga."

He chuckled as he pulled me closer and we continued to dance.

16

I felt her eyes on my back as I left our bed and headed into the bathroom. She'd been too tired to interrogate me or do anything else when we returned home from the party last night, but she seemed bright and alert this morning. I was sure she was going to let me have it...and she did.

"How'd you meet the mayor?" she yelled from the bed.

Standing at the toilet, I smiled. "Uh...through business."

"She was a client?" Her voice was low now, conspiratorial.

"You know I can't tell you that, King."

"And you handled it yourself," she correctly surmised.

"I have no idea what you're talking about," I said as I flushed and moved to the sink. Returning to the bedroom, I approached the bed, reaching for her foot and pulling her to the end of it.

"Now, who was the target?" she mused as I opened her legs and dropped to my knees. "Who—wait, her husband was killed in a robbery. Her whole campaign was centered around being tough on crime because of his death. You killed—ohhhhh, shit!"

I had a mouth full of her pussy at that moment and was torturing her clit with my tongue.

"You...are...so...evilllll!" she wailed.

"Mm-hmm," I hummed as I ate the shit out of her pussy.

Memphis

I WAS SO ready for this, probably a little too ready if I was being honest with myself. More than anything, I needed to be away from Bo for a while to clear my head. Otherwise, I might've started believing we could really be *us* again, and that was downright ridiculous. He and I being a legitimate couple was actual insanity. So was this trip I was taking to Mexico. The route Jerryn had planned was tiring and more than a little stressful, but I trusted it would keep me off the grid and anyone's radar. I needed to get this job done and done right. If anyone deserved to be eliminated, this motherfucker did.

After driving for hours, I was now in a secret compartment of a semi, traveling from Arizona to Mexico. Apparently, the driver owed Jerryn a favor. Someone always owed Jerryn a favor. While I'd spent all my working life ridding the earth of scum, Jerryn had started out rescuing people, liberating cult members and abuse victims—you name it. He couldn't seem to rescue his wife, though. I could relate since I couldn't rescue my own damn self from Bo.

As if I'd conjured up my employee, his voice filled my ear. "You guys are coming up on a checkpoint." He was tracking our movements via GPS and some other tech shit.

I didn't answer, but he knew I could hear him. At that point, he probably could hear my heart racing through the little recording device I wore.

I felt the truck slow to a stop and closed my eyes as I sat in the cramped space. I couldn't wait to get to my accommodations for this trip. I needed to stretch out.

Involuntarily holding my breath, I listened as the rear doors groaned open. Unshuttering my eyes, I focused on the walls around me. The small space I occupied was directly behind the sleeper cab and almost imperceptible. That is, if you weren't *looking* for it. They shouldn't have cared about checking too closely unless they knew to check closely. I hoped they didn't know to. I also hoped the driver was as trustworthy as Jerryn believed him to be.

Shit, shit, shit!

I needed to calm down before one of those dizzy spells hit me and I passed out or something. Jerryn would never put me in danger. Plus, I wasn't getting locked up either way. I'd kill whoever I had to before I let that happen.

Thankfully, I heard the doors shut, and a minute or so later, the truck was moving again.

.   .   .

SENATOR MURRAY HAD BEEN REPRESENTING the people of Texas for eight years. Murray was adored by fellow party members despite polarizing views and a staunch belief that immigrants should be imprisoned right alongside anyone who believed there should be exceptions to strict abortion laws. All this despite having that home in Mexico and ties to human trafficking. The anti-choice rhetoric that was the foundation of the senator's election and re-election campaigns? A fucking joke. If anyone was undercover pro-choice, it was definitely Senator BJ Murray.

Fucking hypocrite.

The senator's property in rural Mexico was located on a huge plot of land and accessed by a dirt road. It was beautiful and sprawling with trees and mountains as its backdrop. The rental car Jerryn secured for me under a fake name was several miles away, as I had switched from it to a bus, a damn motorbike, and finally, my two feet, to get from the tiny apartment I was staying in to the senator's property, arriving at around two in the morning. Jerryn was also in Mexico, and although I couldn't see him, I knew his eyes were on me. He literally had my back.

Now, I was on my haunches in a mango grove a few feet away from the house, eyeing my surroundings, my A.R. in hand. The client advised that the senator awoke early every morning to pick fresh mangos for breakfast.

How quaint.

I waited, the sounds of the night my only company, the air clear, and my concentration acute. The waiting never bothered me. On the contrary, it excited me. While anticipating an elimination, I felt more alive than ever. Alive, alert...predatory. I only hoped some wild animal didn't pop up and I'd have to kill it. I didn't like killing innocent animals.

Around the ungodly hour of 4:00 AM, a light popped on in the house, joining that which was provided by the waxing gibbous moon. I smiled, lifting the rifle as I remained in the shadows of the trees. When I heard a door open and shut, I started feeling something akin to giddiness. Then, a silhouette began to move from the house toward the grove, footsteps sounding against the loose dirt of a path. I didn't move. I didn't flinch. I didn't breathe until the subject was just approaching the perimeter of the grove, and then...pop! I hit her right in the middle of her forehead. Just like that, Senator Bonnie Jean Murray was gone.

I stayed in position, my eyes glued to her lifeless body because I heard...something. I wasn't sure what it was. An animal? Lifting my eyes from the senator, I saw another silhouette in front of the house, a small one.

A child.

Shit.

Fuck!

I knew they couldn't see me dressed in all black to blend in with what remained of the darkness, but what if they came to the grove? They couldn't have heard the silenced shot, but maybe they heard her body drop. What if they discovered the senator's corpse prior to my escape?

Before I could decide what to do, a hand covered my mouth, another yanked me to my feet, and I was being dragged away.

17

Memphis

Then...

I wasn't sure how I felt about this meeting. Was I excited? Annoyed? Angry that I'd been left on read for so long? Did I still have a crush on 11C22? Was it crazy to have a crush on a man I only knew as a set of numbers and a letter?

Probably.

At any rate, I arrived at the restaurant early to find he'd done the same.

"Yes," the hostess chirped after I inquired about the reservation, "right this way."

With my eyes surveying the sparse crowd occupying the space, I followed her to a private room in the back, but the man sitting at the table wasn't 11C22.

I stopped short of him, eyeing him suspiciously. He gave off this vibe, this sinister aura, and I wasn't sure if it intrigued me or alarmed me.

Both?

One thing was for sure; he made me feel *something*, something completely different from the flighty feeling I experienced when I was with the man who recruited me. My cheeks didn't feel warm and there were no butterflies in my belly. From the moment I rested my gaze on this stranger, his smoldering eyes and energy made my heart race as all the blood in my body rushed to my pussy.

I didn't like this feeling.

At all.

His attention was on me, surveying me in silence as I did the same to him.

Oblivious to our exchange, the hostess placed a menu on the table before the empty seat and sang, "Enjoy!" before leaving us alone.

"Who are you?" I demanded once she was gone.

He smiled. "Who are *you*?"

In response, I turned to leave because if he didn't know who the fuck I was, I had no business being there with him.

"Miss King, have a seat," he said.

I spun around to face him. He was okay looking—glasses, neat appearance. Nothing special, but it felt like I was in the room with the damn president or something. He gave off this authoritative ambiance that was almost irresistible. Tightly clutching the strap of my purse, I didn't move.

"Got some pepper spray in there? Gonna get me like you did my brother?"

Brother?

This man was 11C22's brother?

I frowned but remained stationary.

"Or maybe you're going to use some of the moves you learned in my father's self-defense classes."

Father? Now I *knew* he was playing with me. This nigga was a fed or something.

"I think you have me confused with someone else," I stated, my voice even.

He sighed. "Please have a seat so we can talk. This place has been swept for bugs, but I'd like to be able to lower my voice when speaking to you."

I still didn't move.

"Look, I ain't no damn fed. Sit your sexy ass down!" he grunted.

Against my better judgment, I dropped my stupidly-flattered ass into the chair across from him, my eyes never leaving him.

He nodded. "Alert, cautious...my brother said you were good, a true asset to the company. Glad to see he was right."

"Where is he? Why are you here?" I asked.

"Abrupt, callous...I like that, too. No wonder he was so enamored with you."

I blinked, trying not to let his words sidetrack me. "*Where is he?*"

He leaned back in his chair. "There have been some changes in our organization. New management. Me."

"You're what?"

"I'm the new management."

"So...11C22 is fired?"

"No, he's been reassigned. He was getting too personally involved when it came to you. That's bad for business. Although, I see why he did it." He lifted an eyebrow and licked his lips. "So, I'll be your contact from now on."

"You're in management and you're dealing with the help? Why?"

He shrugged. "Because I want to."

"Why contact me now after all this time? Because you were reorganizing or something?"

"That, and I thought it timely to meet you since you decided to kill that doctor."

I froze, my heart throttling my chest. "W-what?" How the fuck did he know about that? I was careful.

"You belong to The Agency. We know your every move. There are always eyes on you."

My mouth opened, but no sound escaped it.

"And I knew this was coming. You don't train to kill without eventually having the desire to kill. It was only a matter of time before you acted on that desire. You did a stellar job, by the way."

"Uh...th-thank you?"

"BUT, let that be the first and last time you do some shit like that. Going rogue could jeopardize our entire operation."

"O...kay."

"Now, let's get down to business. I know you graduated. Congratulations on that. Are you planning to live here?"

"Yes. My family is here, and...thank you again."

"That's fine, but you need a cover."

"Like a job? I've been looking for one."

"We'll set you up with something that looks legit for tax purposes, but in reality, you'll be working for us. We pay through offshore accounts."

"Oh, I don't know..."

"We will handle everything, including tax stuff. So don't worry about that. Second, you'll need to move out of your father's house. Find a place, and we'll take care of the rent."

All I could do was nod.

"Good. On your burner, you'll find the information about your Agency email account and how to access it via the Tor browser. Once you read it, delete the message. Got it?"

"Yes."

"Then that's it." He stood to leave, and I kind of panicked.

"Wait! Aren't you going to tell me who you are?"

"I'm 001A."

Then...

SHE WALKED into that room in that restaurant and birds started chirping and shit. I'd seen pictures and footage of her, so I knew she was fine and pretty as hell, but got damn! In person, the shit was disarming. Those eyes, those lips, those hips?

Jesus Jerome Christ!

This woman was perfection, and when she turned to leave, that ass in those jeans almost made me slide from my chair to my knees. I totally got why Zaccai liked her, but she was too big of an asset for me to let him fuck up her potential. He would've wifed her and taken her off the job, and well, fuck that. We needed someone like her on our roster. Me? I'd wife her and not interfere with her new career.

Damn, was I really thinking about getting with this woman?

Nah, no way I could do that. I had too much going on, too much on my plate to start something with her...

But I wanted to.

Zaccai was pissed when I removed him as her handler, but whatever. He worked better with the guys anyway. Plus, it was my call to make now, since our father was killed.

Fuck.

That hurt. I mean, I wasn't sure if I'd ever get over it. One day he's down in his hometown of Romey, Tennessee, doing his professor and self-defense coach thing while still heading up The Agency, and the next, he's shot dead outside his dojo. My mom was taking it hard, which was crazy since they hadn't lived in the same house in years. I guess love wasn't all that cut and dry.

Now, I was the boss instead of just an agent in my father's company. I'd lived in Parkton for a few years, having relocated after visiting my mom here one Christmas. This was *her* hometown and where she fled when their relationship started crumbling. I missed Chicago, though, where I'd been staying in my childhood home.

"You want her. That's it. First, Ma gives you The Agency, and now you tryna take my woman? I can't have shit!" Zaccai was saying. Hell, I'd zoned out so bad that I forgot we were having a family meeting.

"Zaccai, calm down! You know Bo is already promised to Layla. Plus, that girl is off limits to both of you. She's an employee!" our mother fussed.

Promised to Layla.

That statement fucked my mood completely up.

"Don't look at me like that," my mother directed to me.

I had no idea how I was looking at her, but I assumed my frustration with the whole Layla situation was written all over my face.

"Your father made this agreement to end the war between our family and hers. You know that! You have to follow through with this!" she continued.

Leaning forward at her dining room table, I locked eyes with her. "A war that had nothing to do with me or Layla. That was between my father and hers long before either of us were born. She's a beautiful woman. I'm sure she can marry whoever she wants. She doesn't need this arrangement, and neither do I. I'm not marrying a woman because of some old Chicago street shit."

"I'll marry her," Zaccai offered. "She fine as hell! Bo, you crazy."

"It was more than Chicago street shit, as you put it. That truce kept your father alive, which allowed him and I to create you, and

Zaccai, you know the terms. A son and daughter from opposing fami-lies are to marry. Layla's father only had one child. Your father chose Bo," my mother said.

"But I'm the oldest!" Zaccai whined. This nigga was always whining!

"Her father is old and sick, right? I bet he ain't messed up about that agreement now. That was years ago," I pointed out.

She shook her head. "To men like him and your father, a man's word and honor are everything. He most definitely expects you to marry his daughter, or there will be hell to pay."

I shifted my eyes to the wall behind my mother, scratching my forehead. "Look, this ain't what we're here for, Ma. We covered all the business, so I think this meeting is over."

"Fine, but you *will* marry Layla within the next two years, Bo. What you do between now and then is up to you, but no children. Save that for your marriage," she said.

"I don't even want no damn kids," I told her.

"But you will have children...*with your wife*."

I shook my head before leaving the table and my mother's house.

18

Then...

"How you get an apartment already? You ain't even started this new job, yet!" was how my father responded to my announcement at the dinner table. My sisters looked to be near tears, but neither spoke.

"I just told you, Daddy. I got a sign-on bonus from the company, enough to put down a deposit and get a bed and couch. That's really all I need right now," I replied, adding to the laundry list of lies I'd already told him.

My big bear of a father stared at me, concern and something else in his eyes—fear. "What kind of company you say this is?"

"Mills-Thomas. I'll be working as a pharmaceutical rep for them. I'll be traveling all over, and it's good money, Daddy."

"Healthcare, Memphis? I would think you wouldn't want anything to do with that system after..."

That's when it hit me. Mama. Her loss was why all of them, my family, were taking this news so hard.

So, I stood, abandoning the plate of neck bones and greens "Aunt" Pauline had cooked for us, and stepped around the table to hug my daddy. "I miss her, too, but it's time for me to try to figure life out without her. I'll still be living here in town."

"Not The Village. You said the apartment is in Parkton," he grumbled.

"It's the same thing, Daddy," I reminded him.

"Parkton is changing, getting dangerous in some parts."

"I won't be living in those parts."

"I thought you wanted to be a cop or something."

"I did; maybe I still do. Never said I'd be at this job forever."

Silence from Daddy. Sniffles from Lilith. A hung head from Umber. I moved to hug them, too, but my daddy held onto me, softly saying, "You be careful. You might be mean, but you ain't invincible."

I chuckled. "I will, Daddy. You be careful, too...with Aunt Pauline."

My daddy actually blushed. I was happy he had her around to make him feel better.

My sisters left their seats, and soon, all four of us were locked in a tearful hug. I mean, *I* didn't cry, but they did.

Six months into this new life and I'd already earned fifty thousand dollars from one assignment, an easy one at that. I didn't even have to leave the state, and it helped that the target was this grimy loan shark guy who abused his wife. He had so many enemies, the police would never figure out who shot him in his office late that night. I was in and out in minutes. No witnesses. No evidence left behind. I was really good at this.

So, I was truly taken aback when I answered the door to my relatively new home to find my boss standing there dressed in khakis and a white button-down shirt, brown rimmed glasses, neatly trimmed hair and beard. He was older than me by a few years, but not by that much. I could tell because he had this maturity about him that told me he'd seen and experienced more than I had at that point.

"You gonna let me in, Miss King?" he asked, his voice vibrating in my ears. His energy enveloped me, making me acutely aware of any vulnerabilities I may have possessed even though I couldn't name them. The way he looked at me, the way he smelled? It all made me feel so weak.

I hated it.

"Why are you here?" was how I chose to respond, my eyes glued to his.

He smiled. "This feels a lot like déjà vu, you know?"

Nothing from me.

"You think it would be good to discuss business in your doorway?" he asked.

He did have a point, so I reluctantly let him in, offering him a seat on my couch. I settled on the opposite end of it from him.

"You know, Miss King—" he began, but I cut him off.

"My name is Memphis. Call me Memphis," I said.

"I like King," he replied.

"Well, thank you, but Miss King sounds like an old woman. I'm not an old woman."

"Oh, I know that."

Rolling my eyes, I repeated, "*Why are you here?*"

Turning his body to face mine, he said, "I'm your boss. You're supposed to be nice to me."

"This *is* me being nice."

"Okay, King...just wanted to congratulate you on a job well done. That was a clean extermination."

I nodded. "Yeah, it was."

His laughter was so loud and boisterous that I nearly joined in. "I really like you—the attitude and all. Hell, I might be in love."

I frowned, adjusting my posture to mirror his. "What kind of boss are you? This has got to be illegal, you flirting with an employee."

He flashed another smile which induced another twitch between my thighs. "King, this whole company is built on illegality."

He did have a point...again.

Scanning the living room, he shared, "Looks good in here. I like what you've done with the place."

"Thank you. So...you came here to do a performance evaluation? That's it?"

He stared at me as if making a decision. Then he said, "Come here," in this low voice. Not exactly commanding but not begging, either. Rather, it felt beseeching and full of deep desire. And damned if I didn't want to obey him. I wasn't the obeying type when it came to men or much of anyone else because fuck that. So, I didn't move... although I wanted to.

Instead, I asked, "Why?"

He licked his nice lips, his eyes darkening. "Because I said so, King."

"You might be my boss, but you don't own me. You can't make me do shit, Mr. 001A."

"Bo."

That one word made my heart jolt in my chest. "What?"

"My name is Bo. That's what I want you to call me." He moved closer to me, the scent of him crawling all over me. "When I finally fuck you, I wanna hear you scream that, not some damn numbers."

I blinked hard as he moved even closer. "I'm not fucking you. To be honest, I don't even like you. You can fire me if that's going to be a problem."

His face was mere centimeters from mine as he countered, "You don't like me, but you're damn near hyperventilating, King. Don't worry, I won't touch you today—"

Some crazy bitch inside me jumped out and kissed this nigga, hard and rough. He was so caught off guard that he moaned in what had to be an uncharacteristic and momentary show of weakness. He kissed me back, matching my vigor, and when we parted, we just sat there, our heaving breaths crashing in the small space between us. What seemed like a millennia later, he pecked my lips one soft time, before wordlessly leaving my sofa and my home.

My only thought?

Why the fuck did I do that?

19

Memphis

Now...

I was dragged through the grove into the trees beyond the house. There, I was warned, "I'm going to let you go. Don't run or scream," as if I didn't already know not to do that. I'd just killed a sitting US senator. I wasn't trying to get caught!

Once free, I hit him upside his damn head with my fist before backing up to kick him in the gut.

"Damn," he grunted, holding his stomach. "This how you greet a nigga?"

"You lucky I didn't shoot your stupid ass! Bo, what the fuck are you doing here?!" I said through clenched teeth. "I am working, fool!"

"I saw. Good, clean kill, by the way."

I dropped my shoulders. "I saw someone standing outside the house. A kid, maybe. A-a witness."

"You're that kid's hero. That was one of her victims."

I nodded. "I figured that. I just...shouldn't we go back and help them? What if there are others? What if some other ass-wipe swoops in and sells them or something?"

"The authorities will be contacted as soon as we get out of here. Speaking of which, let's go. We're running out of time."

He grasped my hand, leading me deeper into the canopy of trees until we reached what looked to be a shack. By then, the sun was beginning to creep into the sky. I watched as he opened the door, pulling me into the dark structure.

"There's a ladder that leads down into a tunnel. This is how they move the kids," he said, pointing to a wide hole in the floor in the middle of the one-room shack.

I gasped, "What?"

"We gotta hurry, baby. No time to discuss this."

I nodded, observing as he descended the ladder. I decided to close the door before following him with my rifle slung over my shoulder. We both wore gloves—an essential part of our uniform—so I knew we wouldn't leave any fingerprints behind. Then again, a place used to illegally transport people would probably be a nightmare to investigate—fingerprints everywhere.

Once I hit the bottom of the ladder, I was assaulted by an odor that had to come from bodily waste. It almost took my breath away, but I held it together, following Bo and his flashlight as he moved forward.

The tunnel was tight but tall enough that we didn't have to crawl, probably to accommodate the kidnappers who accompanied the victims to prevent any escapes. It was stuffy, dank, dark, and I had to keep resisting the urge to use my own flashlight to check behind us to see if we were being followed when I knew we weren't. We walked for what felt like ten hours before Bo stopped at another ladder and just stood there.

"What are you—" I began, but he shushed me, which almost made me shoot his ass for real. No one shushed me.

No one.

We stood there for I know a good thirty minutes waiting on God knows what or who before I heard a scraping sound and dim light shone on his beautiful face.

He smiled, blinking against the light. Reaching for my hand, he said, "You go first."

I frowned and didn't move a muscle. "Who-what's up there?"

"Safety. Go! I'm right behind you, baby."

As much as I hated when he called me that, it did give me some comfort. After all, he wouldn't let something happen to his "baby" would he?

Shit, *would he?*

Fuck it. I got a big ass gun, I thought, a*nd I'm good at using it.*

Taking Bo's place at the ladder, I began climbing it, my muscles sore from all the walking in combination with the anxiety that was plaguing me. I wanted out of this tunnel and this country before some shit popped off. I was also hungry and tired and beginning to feel light-headed.

Shit.

Once I made it to the top, a hand appeared, reaching to help me. I hesitantly took it, emerging from the darkness to find myself in the middle of a damn desert. The hand belonged to a man I'd never seen before. Tall, olive skin, kind of handsome. He still held my hand when Bo joined us above ground.

"Motherfucker, let her fucking hand go!" Bo bellowed.

"Shit, sorry. Just making sure she's okay. That's all," the man said after dropping my hand like it was boiling hot.

Bo snarled at him before turning his attention to me. "You good? He hurt you gripping your hand and shit?"

I shook my head, which was a mistake because it seemed to knock something loose in my skull. Before I could reassure him of my well-being, I felt myself sinking to the ground...and everything went black.

20

Memphis

I awoke in a dimly lit room. I was on a bed, and the only sound I heard was a hum. My ears felt full, and my stomach felt empty. My body just felt...tired.

"Hey," came a voice that belonged to a familiar energy.

"You were following me? Watching me?" I asked, my eyes to the ceiling, my hand cradling my forehead.

"I'm always watching you. Always making sure you're safe," he told me.

I turned to see him sitting next to the bed, disquiet in his eyes. "I can take care of myself."

He nodded, leaning forward, his eyebrows in a tangle. "I know that. I do it for my own peace of mind because I love you."

Returning my attention to the ceiling, I queried, "How long have you been watching me?"

"For The Agency? Since you joined. For me? Since the first time I met you face to face."

"So, you're trying to say you've loved me that long? Bullshit."

"You know I have."

Nothing from me.

"King, what's going on with you? Why'd you pass out?" he probed, pissing me off.

"Because I walked miles in a dark, dank, disgusting-ass tunnel with no food or water! Isn't that obvious?" I spat.

Shaking his head, he said, "Nah, it's more than that. I know you. I know your body. Something is off. Something's *been* off."

"*Now* you wanna be concerned? You weren't concerned when you decided to take me hostage."

"I ain't doing shit to you that you don't want done. If you didn't want to be with me, if you didn't *love* me, you would've killed my ass by now."

"You ain't worth the trouble."

"Mm-hmm."

"And if you're so worried, why didn't you take me to a doctor?"

"I brought one to you. Your vitals were fine. He said you probably just needed rest."

"See? Exactly."

"I wanna hear what your regular doctor has to say."

"Where are we going?" I asked. Finally realizing we were on The Agency's jet.

"Home, baby."

I sighed, and then a thought hit me. "Shit, Jerryn—"

Bo held up a hand while dialing a number on his phone with the other. I could hear it ring, heard Jerryn answer.

"Proof of life, as promised. Here she is. I've been taking care of her, just like I told you I would," Bo said into the phone before handing it to me.

I stared at him until he got the message and left the room.

Once I was alone, the words fell out of my mouth. "Jerryn, I don't know what the fuck is going on. I made the kill and Bo showed up and accosted me and—"

"You were set up. I told you this felt too easy. I got word from a source that the senator's illegal business partners were on their way to eliminate *you*. Bo Pierce got you out of there just in time."

"What? Why would...they're the client?"

"Looks like it."

"Damn. Oh! There was a child there. They might've seen me. I don't know..."

"Don't worry. As soon as I realized what was going on, I contacted the authorities—anonymously, of course. The kids were all rescued. The partners were taken into custody. None of the kids have said anything about seeing you. It was dark. You had on black, as usual. You're being paranoid."

"Can you blame me?"

"No. When I lost track of you, I fucking panicked, and then your guy contacted me, and I was like what the hell is going on and how the fuck did he get my number? Anyway, he said you'd been in a tunnel and that's why I couldn't track you. The whole thing is protected from signals, air tags, all of it."

"Wow. I just don't know what to say."

"Shit, me either. Hey, are you okay, Raja? You fainted?"

"I'm...I'm fine."

"I don't think you are, and this job is too dangerous to lie to yourself about something like this. I'm not working another job with you until you get checked out."

I bolted up in the bed and instantly regretted it. I was dizzy as hell and extra pissed off about it. "Are you threatening me? Let's not forget who pays who!"

"Yeah, you *do* pay me, but you're also someone I care about. I don't want anything to happen to you. You can't be around freezing and fainting like this."

I was silent for a moment, so he said, "Raja? Boss?"

"I gotta go. I'll be in touch," I said, ending the call before he could respond. Falling back on the bed, I clutched Bo's phone tightly in my hand and squeezed my eyes shut, opening them when I heard him return to the room.

"You hungry?" he asked.

"Yes," I croaked.

He nodded and turned to leave but stopped when I called his name.

Facing me again, he raised his eyebrows. "Yeah?"

I swallowed hard, dropping my gaze from his face. "Come here."

He moved, sitting on the side of the bed, his head angled toward me.

"No, lie down with me," I said.

His eyes filled with a combination of surprise and so much affection that it almost made mine mist. Then he joined me in the bed, pulling my body into his. I closed my eyes and let him. I let him comfort me because I was fucking scared.

Then...

I KEPT FINDING MYSELF HERE, at her place, and she kept letting me come inside, if hesitantly. We usually spent a good amount of time arguing—her asking why I kept bothering her and me asking why she kept *letting* me bother her.

"You're my boss. Didn't know I had a choice," was her answer this time.

I laughed. "You don't give a shit about me being your boss. You know that, and I know that."

She shrugged, a little smile playing on her pretty lips.

"You like me. Admit it," I teased her.

With a dramatic eye roll, she replied, "I hate you. You know that. I liked your brother, though. He was nice."

I involuntarily flinched. "A nice assassin? That shit don't even make sense."

She grinned, turning her body to fully face me. "You're jealous."

"Of my brother? HELL no. He ain't nobody to be jealous of."

"Why not? He's taller than you, he's very handsome, he has a personality, he—"

"Why you ain't kiss him like you been kissing me, then?"

Tilting her head to the right, she posed, "How do you know I didn't?"

"Because I know. Plus, Zaccai's lame ass would've told me. He was really feeling you. He ain't have no idea what to do with you, though."

She reclined her neck. "And you do?"

"I know *exactly* what to do with *and* to you, and I'ma do it all as soon as you decide to let me."

"So, you know your brother likes me and you're still tryna screw me? Really? No code of honor? No family loyalty?"

"When it comes to a woman like you? Nope. Like I said, he wouldn't know what to do with you. Y'all don't match."

"What does that mean?"

"It means, me and you? We got the same mind, the same energy."

"I ain't evil like you!"

"But you're attracted to my evil ass, ain't you? With me, you feel things you never felt with my brother. Admit it."

"I ain't admitting SHIT."

I laughed. "You're so fucking mean and I love it."

She frowned, shifting her gaze to the wall across from us. "So, all these visits is you working up to fucking me?"

"Yes and no. I definitely wanna fuck you, but that ain't all I want. I want your heart."

She stared at me before *she* started laughing, stopping when she saw that I wasn't joining her.

"Wait, you're serious? You want like a relationship with me or something? Seriously? Like, for real?" she inquired.

I nodded. "Why wouldn't I? You're everything I've ever wanted in a woman—beautiful, fine, smart, a killer..."

She fixed her eyes on me, wordlessly inspecting my face. Then she moved from her seat, scooting closer to me.

Holding my face in her hands, she softly kissed me and said, "I know *I'm* a catch, but why in the fuck would I want to be in a relationship with you?"

I grinned. "*You* tell *me*. Why do you want me, King?"

She rolled her eyes before kissing me again while climbing into my lap and grinding on me.

My dick was already harder than a got damn steel construction beam, had been since she opened her front door. But her body? It was a fucking work of art with clothes on. Once she left my lap and undressed, I knew for sure I was going to lose my mind over her. Thick thighs, wide hips, big juicy ass breasts, a booty made for gripping.

This shit didn't make no sense!

She stood over me, naked, her eyes below my waist, and I had to ask myself why the fuck I was still sitting on her sofa with my damn clothes on. The hell was wrong with me?

I remedied that problem by hopping up and quickly dropping my slacks and underwear. She removed my shirt and kissed my chest, her tongue dragging over my nipples, I had to suppress the chill that ran through me. She was twenty-two to my twenty-nine. I wasn't going to go out like a much younger amateur. I had a point to prove. When I got done with her ass, she wasn't ever going to want another man.

When she lifted her head to kiss me, I grasped her hand, dropping back onto the couch and pulling her down to straddle my lap again. We kissed and moaned as she stroked me and I slid my fingers inside her heat. So hot, so fucking tight...I couldn't wait to be inside her.

"Condom," she murmured against my mouth.

"Wallet," I muttered.

She left my lap, and I wanted to beg her to come back but opted to watch as she dug in my pants pocket and retrieved my wallet, opening it. When she froze, I frowned.

"What's wrong?" I asked, mentally adding, *please don't say you changed your mind because I gots to fuck you. God knows I do.*

"Your driver's license...your name is Mephibosheth?" she inquired.

Shit, hearing my full first name almost made my dick deflate.

"Damn, you pronounced it right," I observed.

She shrugged one shoulder, giving me a grin. "Lucky guess."

I nodded, eyeing her body. "You gon' get the condom or..."

"Right! Your middle initial is T? What's that stand for?"

"I'll tell you once I'm inside you."

She quickly found a condom and returned to me, watching as I covered myself with it. Then...paradise. I was inside her, my hands gripping her ass as she rode me with her head thrown back, displaying her neck and breasts. I sucked the flesh of her neck, moved my hands to palm her breasts and pinch her nipples.

"Shit!" I screamed because how the fuck could she possibly feel this good?

Her moans were virtually continuous as she rode me, her mouth agape, head still collapsed between her shoulder blades. I wished I could paint or had a camera handy or something. I needed to capture the moment, freeze this view of her, so beautiful and totally free. I knew I was going to fall in love with her if I hadn't already. Shit, I wasn't sure since I'd never been in love before. I'd been in lust, for sure, but love? If it was real, I somehow knew I would and could only experience it with the beautiful Memphis King.

"Ohhhhh! Oh-oh-oh!!!" she wailed as her walls began to shudder around me.

In turn, my balls started to tingle as I clenched my ass and felt the building nut release. "Oh, fuck! Tidal! My middle name is mother-fucking Tidal!" I grunted.

I dropped my head onto the back of the couch while trying to catch my breath, eyes closed, chest heaving as I continued to grip her ass.

I was in a nice haze when I heard her say, "Tidal? What kind of middle name is that?"

Opening one eye, I replied, "Better than my brother's. That nigga's name is Zaccai Tiberius."

"Damn."

21

Memphis

Now...

When we returned from Mexico, he took me to my apartment instead of his house and basically moved in with me. So, I was still his captive.

Whatever.

There I lay in my bed, watching him sleep like he owned the whole damn world.

He definitely owns your ass, I thought.

I hated my thoughts, not that they were inaccurate.

"Why you staring at me?" he mumbled, startling me. "Over there acting like you love me or something." Opening an eye, he offered me a lazy grin.

"Trying to figure out how you can be so damn evil and sleep so soundly. Like, you really think I won't dispatch you, huh?"

Rolling over to face me, his smile widened. "I *know* you won't."

Still observing him, I reached behind me, grabbing the little twenty-two I kept on my bedside table and placing it against his forehead. "You sure about that?"

He reached up, moving my hand and pulling my body closer to his. "I'm certain of it."

I stared at him for a moment before saying, "Thank you for saving me. Jerryn told me I was in danger."

"I got you. I'ma always have your back. Believe that."

"I...I do."

He softly kissed my lips before advising, "Put on something nice. They'll be here in about thirty minutes."

I frowned. "Who?"

"You'll see," he threw over his shoulder as he left the bed.

"And how you gon' invite someone to *my* place?"

He stepped into my en-suite bathroom without bothering to reply.

THIS CAN'T BE REAL.

And he can't be serious.

Because...what the fuck?

Just when I started thinking maybe he wasn't as much of a dick as I believed him to be, he pulled this shit.

Son of a bitch!

Literally.

"You have got to be playing!" I shouted, sitting on the side of my bed in one of my best outfits. It was a wrap-style dress in a bright shade of red and I looked good in it, but if I'd known I was dressing for my funeral, I would've chosen some sackcloth or something.

Standing over me with his arms crossed at his chest, he shook his big-ass head with a stupid-ass smile on his dumb-ass face. "No, I'm not playing. This is part of our agreement, remember? I saved your sister's life, and you agreed to—"

"How can you profess to love me and actually hold me to an agreement I made out of desperation?!"

"Easily. Come on," he ordered, proffering me his hand.

I knocked it away and stood, stalking to the bedroom door with his laughter following me.

Once in my living room, my stomach dropped. This shit was really happening. Like, for real.

"I would've invited your family, but I figured you wouldn't want me to," Bo said, his mouth on my ear.

"Definitely not."

"You wanna call Jerryn and have him come over?"

"No. Why is the Mexico Italian here?" I asked, referring to the man who helped me out of the tunnel. He was standing in front of my wall-mounted TV wearing a shiny black suit with a damn gun in one hand and a book in the other. Was that a...Bible?

"Right! You passed out and shit before I could introduce y'all. King, this is Gianluca, also known as 75GL. He's an Agency vet like you, and the lady sitting on the sofa is his wife, Jessi, or 4D22. She's been with us for a while, too."

Despite my distress, I could see that the tall, handsome Gianluca and petite, chocolate-skinned Jessi made for a gorgeous couple as they both smiled and greeted me. Jessi wore a demure pink dress and had a forty-five cradled in her hands.

"Okay, now I know his name, but why is he here? Why are *they* here?" I asked.

"Gianluca got ordained just for this occasion. He'll be officiating. Jessi is our witness," Bo informed me.

"Don't we need a license or something?" I questioned him.

"It's sitting over on the kitchen counter waiting for your signature," he said.

I didn't bother asking how he got one without me being present. I mean, did it really matter?

My stomach gurgled as Bo grasped my hand and nodded at the Italian. "We're ready."

Gianluca said, "Gotcha, boss. Uh...shit, let me put this down." Then he placed his gun on my lovely glass coffee table with a painful *ping*.

"You got me, baby?" he directed to his wife who tapped her gun in response.

Good Lord. What the fuck kind of wedding was this?

"Okay, so...we're gathered here to join this man and this woman in holy matrimony. Uh, I'ma skip some of this script, Boss. That okay with you? Me and the missus gotta head back home to the kids, know-what-I-mean?" the Italian asked in the thickest New York accent I'd ever heard in my life.

"Yep, got it," Bo affirmed.

"All right, so Boss, do you take her as your wife?"

"I do," Bo said loud and proud.

Ugh.

"And Miss Boss, do you take him as your husband?" Gianluca asked me.

"Hell no," I said under my breath, causing Bo to squeeze the fucking life out of my hand.

"Ow! Damn! Yes, I do!" I shrieked.

"You can put the rings on your fingers and shit," our officiant advised us.

Bo dug three rings out of the front pocket of his black slacks, handing his to me. The bridal set he slid onto my left ring finger was nice and expensive looking.

As was right and proper.

In kind, I slid the simple platinum band onto his finger.

"Okay, so boom! You's married and shit! You can kiss the bride, Boss!"

In response, Bo kissed me so long and hard and deep that I almost forgot my damn name.

22

After she acted like she didn't want to marry me, I drove us to the airport to board my jet. No security, just me and my wife flying off to our honeymoon spot. She was quiet, probably a little regretful, but I didn't give a shit. This was what she wanted, what she'd always wanted, whether she was willing to admit it to me or not.

"Where'd you say we're going?" she asked, her eyes still outside the window.

"It's a surprise," I answered.

"I don't like surprises."

"I know, but you'll be a'ight. You're gonna like this one."

She huffed, and I smiled.

"Hey, when you gonna tell your family?" I queried.

She finally gave me her full attention. "Same time you tell yours. I'm sure Mama Pierce will be elated."

Cocking my head to the side, I said, "I don't give a fuck how she or anybody else feels about it. Not their business."

"Hmm," she hummed as she returned her gaze to the window. "I wish you'd felt that way back in the day. Might've saved me a lot of heartache."

"I...didn't have a choice. You know that. I never wanted to marry Layla. I never loved her."

"But you made a baby with her after telling me you didn't want any children."

"I didn't. Still don't."

"So, it just...'happened'?"

"Actually, yes."

"And your son?"

"What about him?"

She shook her head while releasing a wry chuckle. "Okay."

"King, don't try to start some shit with me. This is our honeymoon, and I'ma enjoy it *and you*."

"You're going to keep calling me King now that you've forced your name on me?"

"I ain't force shit. You ain't gotta take my name. You're my wife, regardless."

She was silent, which made a thought hit me.

"Oh, wait. You wanna take my last name, don't you?" I posed.

"Fuck you," she softly uttered.

"I got you, Mrs. Pierce."

Without turning to look at me, she gave me her middle finger, and I laughed.

Memphis

I FELL asleep on the plane and was disoriented when he awakened me hours later.

"You need to eat," he said, nodding toward the air hostess standing over us holding a tray.

Frowning, I nodded, letting my eyes travel back to the window. It was dark now.

Once the food was set in front of us on a table and the hostess had disappeared, I asked, "How much longer is the flight? Where the hell are we going? Antarctica?"

He grinned. "Again, it's a surprise. You good with the food? I know you like seafood. Made sure to have your favorite wine stocked on here, too."

Paying attention to the food for the first time, I felt my mouth begin to water. Mussels, calamari, shrimp—damn! Plus, a micro greens salad. He knew I would love this.

"It'll do," I mumbled.

Through a chuckle, he said, "You are so full of shit."

Involuntarily, I smiled.

WE LANDED IN BEAUTIFUL ZANZIBAR, a place I'd never visited before, although I had taken a few trips to other countries on the continent. I kept at least two passports on me—one real and one not so real, but no Visa. Yet, we somehow didn't need one. Watching how the people in the immigration office interacted with Bo, I quickly figured he had a government connect, probably a former client. We had to take a car and then a boat to make it to our final destination—Thanda Island. This part of the Zanzibar archipelago was privately owned, and we had the entire island to ourselves save for a small staff, according to Bo. This shit had to have a crazy price tag on it.

And it was breathtaking!

Surrounded by turquoise waters and adorned with a gorgeous beach and striking greenery, this relatively small island was truly paradise.

As I followed Bo into the main villa, as he described it, I felt... good? Happy? Was it safe to feel happy with this man? Shit, were we safe here at all?

As if he read my thoughts, he informed me, "There's security on the island, by the way."

"Good," I said, "since you've been ducking Moody and the rest of his crew lately."

After he instructed the butler to take our bags to the bedroom, he cupped my face in his hands and kissed my forehead. "You're worried about my safety, baby? Such a good wife."

Snatching away from him, I snapped, "I just don't wanna get blamed for someone offing you."

He licked his lips and slowly nodded. "Riiiiight. Anyway, I have my own security, they just know how to be inconspicuous. My mom wants Moody up my ass to keep tabs on me for her."

"Hmm, so you moving to my apartment was a way of ducking him, too, wasn't it?"

"Not really. Motherfucker couldn't even keep up with me to know I was in Mexico. Hell, I don't think he's really trying anymore."

"I see, well...this is nice." I let my eyes round the open-air sitting area with a relaxing view of the beach.

"Anything for my lovely wife," he cooed.

For the millionth time, I rolled my eyes.

23

Then...

"Y ou really like this weird shit, huh?" I asked as I squeezed her closer to me in the bed.

"Yes! You like *The X-Files*, too, don't you?" she replied, pushing her ass against my dick.

"Why you say that?"

"Well, one: you're watching it right now, and two: your dick is rock hard."

"I'm watching it because *you're* watching it, and my dick is hard because your naked ass is touching it."

"We just had sex, Bo."

"And?"

"Wow."

"Ain't my fault you got good pussy."

"Hmph, and folks say hysterectomy pussy ain't good."

"Who said that shit?"

"My mom, or at least she said that's what she was told growing up...that it's dry or something. She was so upset when she had to have one, not that it saved her."

"Sorry about your mom, King. For real. Losing a parent hurts like hell. I don't think I'll ever get over losing my dad. He wasn't perfect, but he loved his family."

She flipped over, her eyes wide, Scully and Mulder forgotten. "Wait, Riley is dead?! Since when?!"

I hadn't brought it up before because I was just kind of getting past it. Nevertheless, I said, "A few months back. That's why I'm running The Agency. I took his place."

"Oh, wow. I liked him. He didn't seem too evil."

"He is—*was* a good actor. I got this shit from him."

"What happened?"

"Got mugged and shot outside his dojo. Fucked up, ain't it?"

"Very fucked up! How did someone manage to get the jump on him? He was...I don't know. Seems impossible."

"Yeah...I don't know how it happened, either. I don't get it."

"Hmm...so, it's just you and your brother? You're the oldest, right?"

"Nah, Zaccai is the oldest; he just don't act like it."

"Zaccai. His first name is waaaaay better than yours."

"Fuck you, King."

"What? He looks better, too. I told you that."

"What you doing in my arms right now, then? Why you ain't in his?"

"I don't know. I think you hexed me or something."

"Nah, that nigga don't turn you on like I do. Admit it."

"Whatever."

"*And*, you like the power you know I have."

She hopped right over that statement. "So, Riley's last name was really Pierce?"

"No, it was Riley. Me and Zaccai got our mother's last name. They were never legally married, although they said they were. It was a way to protect the money, but they loved each other, just couldn't get along for shit outside of business. My parents didn't have the fairytale yours did."

"Yeah...well, it ended like a fairytale, a *real* one. Not the ones they've modified for kids. The cradle fell and my mom died."

"Sorry...again."

"I'm sorry about your dad, too."

"Tell me about your mom."

"You already know all about her. I know you've researched her."

"I don't mean facts anyone could know. Tell me about who she was to you...her daughter."

She sighed, her eyes downcast. "She was so beautiful, like otherworldly so. So wise and magnetic. Her laugh was contagious; her humor was unmatched. She was such a good mother. Stern, caring, and accommodating all at the same time. I will never stop missing her."

"She sounds like an angel."

"She was."

"So are you. A dangerous one."

She smiled, and we both laughed. Then we stared at each other in her bedroom with the black furniture, the only light provided by the small TV on her dresser. She kissed me, and I kissed her back.

"By the way, they definitely lied about the dry pussy thing. Your shit is like a kiddie pool," I said.

"Shut your stupid ass up," she replied through a giggle.

I'd never heard her mean ass giggle before. It was nice.

"Hey, I love you," I told her.

Her eyes met mine, and after a moment of hesitation, she admitted, "I think I love you, too."

Memphis

Then...

IT'S weird how love works, how it hits you, how it fills you, how undeniable it is, and I desperately wanted to deny it. Bo Pierce was a walking red flag—cocky with interstellar dick. Hell, three months into this little relationship and I was terribly addicted to him, wanting to be with him every second of every day, and I'd never been fatalistic about men. I filed them in a place that kept me focused on my goals, but I guess that didn't apply to this situation. I had the degree, the apartment, a job, and enough money to buy anything I wanted. I'd accomplished my goals, even the law enforcement one. I made a practice of only accepting jobs where exterminating the client would make the world a better place. Due process can be a hindrance to justice. I was able to dole out my own due process, and as wrong as it was, it seemed right when the target was an evil piece of shit, but weren't Bo Pierce and his family evil? They recruited me and trained me to be a killer while I was in college, and now, at twenty-three, I was still very green and extremely wet behind the ears and I knew it. Yet, I wasn't compelled to stop, to quit. Honestly, I might've been young, but I did have sense enough to know it wouldn't be as easy as putting in a two-week notice. The Agency specialized in murder, albeit a very glamorous form of it. If I was allowed to quit, I was sure I'd never feel safe with the knowledge of the company I held. Add to that the fact I'd gotten myself entangled with the boss, and I knew I was in too deep. He'd shared his real name along with those of his brother and mother with me rather than just sticking to coded identities. I knew about the inner workings of the establishment, the hierarchy, the security measures used, all of it shared during pillow talk. He trusted me, and that was a big deal.

"I want you to meet my mom," he said as we sat on my living room floor eating Chinese food.

I stopped chewing my chow mein, giving him my attention. He looked...determined, as if he knew I would refuse but was dead set on changing my mind.

"Why?" I garbled. It was all I could think to say.

"Because she needs to meet the woman I'm going to marry."

24

Now...

I needed a fucking camera, a fancy paparazzi one because I was sure the one on my phone wouldn't adequately capture the beauty of my current view. As I sat on the lounger situated on the beach, I watched my wife's naked form wade into the ocean. I'd long ago memorized every curve, dimple, and scar on her body, but I never got tired of looking at it. We'd finally reached a goal I set for us long ago—marriage. It took longer than I could've ever imagined, but I kept my promise. I was hers, even if she believed she didn't want me when I knew she did. I also understood her hesitance. I understood why she didn't trust me anymore, and I was willing to spend every second of the rest of my life proving to her just how much I loved her, that she was all that mattered to me, that I would raze the entire world for her.

On everything, I would.

I didn't like most people. Many days, I couldn't even stand *myself*, but this woman reached into my chest and grabbed my heart that day at the restaurant, never letting it go. I loved her.

I loved her.

I truly did.

She left the water, the sun kissing her pretty brown skin as she made her way back to her lounger, or at least I thought that was her destination. Instead, she approached mine, lifting one shapely leg to straddle me. I moved to sit up, but she pushed against my chest, stopping me. Water rolled off her body onto mine as she leaned in to kiss me.

Once our mouths parted, I murmured, "You just don't know how much I love you."

She sat up, her naked pussy resting right on my erection, the fabric of my swimming trunks the only barrier between us.

"I think I believe you," she admitted.

Reaching up, I laid a hand on her cheek and felt my dick twitch when she leaned into my touch. "I finally convinced you, huh?"

"No, *I* convinced me. I realized you never stopped. You're just...I don't know. It's hard, Bo. I mourned us for years. It's hard to believe this will last."

"I'ma *make* it last. I'll die before I lose you again. I'll self-dispatch before I let that happen."

Her eyes widened. "Bo..."

I shook my head. "I ain't say that to be dramatic. Shit is the truth. I mourned, too. I never got over losing you. Never stopped wanting you back. I didn't bother you, stopped myself from killing those dudes you messed with. I was tryna do right by you, but I can't do that shit again."

My wife wasn't one for crying, but she did show emotion in other ways. In this instance, she showed it by damn near ripping my trunks off me and sheathing my dick in her snugness, making me moan from the bottom of my ass. She felt so good that I swear I could feel my mind leaving me. Closing my eyes, I grasped her hips, holding her as I slammed up into her. All the time I spent in the fucking gym and paying a chef to cook healthy shit paid off when it came to this. I had the stamina and strength to fuck my wife every hour on the hour. I also had the desire to do it because what she had between her legs was divine, mystical, and magically delicious.

"Ohhh, fuck!" I groaned. "Get up, baby."

"I don't wanna stop," she whined.

"I know," I panted. "I want you in the sand...on your knees."

Without another word, she sucked in a breath as she lifted from my body, allowing me to ease out of her. Seconds later, her knees and elbows were in the sand, her ass in the air, and my dick was leaking like I'd just hit puberty. Joining her in the sand, I gripped her ass and slid into her.

"Got damn! Don't nothing in the world feel as good as this!" I declared, and I wasn't lying.

She whimpered in response, the smooth skin of her back calling on me to kiss it. So, I did, my stomach quivering as I moved inside her. Her heat, her pussy's grip on my dick, and her wetness worked together to make me prematurely bust, but I managed to stave off an unwanted ending by pulling out intermittently to lick her asshole and finger her pussy. With a thumb in her ass, I fucked her until I was sure the only logical conclusion would be a heart attack for me, and when it was all over, I collapsed onto my back and tried not to hyperventilate.

"You're gonna get sand in your ass crack," Memphis said, her voice baring a lazy, post-sex tone.

"Mm-hmm—shit!"

Out of nowhere, her mouth was on me, and all I could do was mewl like a damn bitch.

Memphis

"MARRIED?!" Lilith literally screamed into the phone. "When? How? To who? Where are you? What?!"

"You married Kylo Ren?" Umber inquired; her voice was much calmer than Lilith's.

"Shiiiid, I didn't even think this was possible. Is it that Moteezosket boy?" my daddy asked.

I'd decided to call Lilith and have her conference in Daddy and Umber while Bo was in the shower, but I was now regretting it.

"Yes, Daddy. It's Bo," I said.

"I don't even know what the negro do for a living and you done married him?" Daddy complained.

"He has a very good job working for a tech company," I informed him.

"Well, I knew he had to be special to deal with your hateful self. You happy?" Daddy probed.

"Yes," I admitted because at that moment, I was.

"Wow! Damn, I'm the only single King sister left," Umber said.

"Uh, congratulations, but I feel some kind of way about you not inviting us to the wedding," Lilith said.

"Wasn't much of a wedding. Happened in my living room, and it was very spontaneous."

"Uh-huh. We gotta have a get together to celebrate y'all. You say you on your honeymoon?" That was Daddy.

"Yes. On an island. It's beautiful," I said as I watched Bo towel off while entering the bedroom. He smiled when his eyes met mine and walked over to where I lay on the bed to kiss me.

"You know his family?" Umber asked.

"He got family?" Ray interjected. When did his ass get on the phone?

"Yes, and yes. Look, I've gotta go. I'll talk to y'all later."

After ending the call, I placed my cell on the nightstand and stared at my husband's body. In truth, he was far from average. He was fine as hell, and the aging process had been very kind to him. Shit, at fifty-four, he was healthier than men half his age.

"Damn," I muttered under my breath as he turned to face me, towel discarded. Every chiseled muscle of his chest and abdomen taunted me.

"What?" he asked, his eyebrows furrowed. He was so damn hand-some—smooth mocha skin, deep-set eyes, luscious lips. He gave Denzel a run for his money.

"Oh, I didn't say anything," I lied.

He chuckled and shook his head as he pulled his black briefs on. "For such an efficient killer, you're a lousy ass liar, King."

I tossed my middle finger up at him and had to smile at the way he burst into laughter.

MY GUARD WAS ALL the way down for the first time in years, probably for the first time since my mother passed. No, I felt like this when I was with Bo before...until I didn't. Until the bond we so swiftly built was destroyed.

Squeezing my eyes shut, I leaned into him as we swayed in the moonlight, my toes digging in the sand. There was no music, just Bo's soft humming as we danced. He had a nice singing—or humming—voice.

It was our last night in our private paradise, and I honestly didn't want it to end. We'd eaten the best food, meals full of exotic dishes. We made the best love. We lived with no thoughts of anything but us. It almost made me wish this could've been our past, but I can admit I was happy it was our present.

"Bo?" I whispered, my voice so soft and demure that it actually startled me.

It must have taken him aback as well because he stopped moving, backing away a little to look into my eyes. "What's wrong, baby?"

"I need to know something."

He nodded, reaching for my hand and leading me to the villa's massive back patio. Once he'd taken a seat in a chair, he pulled me down onto his lap and said, "What do you want to know?"

"If you love me, why would you let my sister die? You say you've loved me all these years, so why didn't you cancel the order and put the word out without me having to negotiate with you?"

He tried to squeeze me close to his chest, but I resisted. "No. Tell me because if Ray hadn't fallen in love with her, she'd be dead!" I was trembling at that point, a mixture of pure anger and frustrating confusion.

"I honestly didn't know at first. You know I have staff that handles the parts of the process that aren't automated. I don't know about every single target unless they think I need to," he explained.

"You know about all of my targets. You say you've been watching me since day one."

"You're the only thing I care about. Of course, I know all your targets."

"Then you should've been keeping tabs on the people I love, too! You should've known I wouldn't want anything to happen to them!"

"Okay, I'll admit that my loyalty is extremely myopic. When I say it's only you that I care about, I mean it. I don't even give a fuck about my own family, but know this: as soon as you contacted me about it, I kept my eye on the situation. I didn't contact the client because I knew they'd just move on and hire someone else, but I looked into it, figured out Ray was protecting her. So, I knew she was safe."

"But you reassigned her hit!"

"Yeah, I did. To me! It was my way of working around the systems built into the company. You know all cases that aren't handled in a timely manner automatically get reassigned. I preempted that. Then, I put out the word that she was off limits...before you asked me to."

"You...what? I don't believe it."

"I can prove it. I can show you the database, the records, everything I have access to. I can give you the fucking passwords and you can see it all. Hell, it's all yours anyway...wife."

The first tear fell unbidden, the ones that followed, too. The only thing I did purposely was kiss him, fall into his arms, and utter words that had been bottled up inside me for damn near three decades.

"I love you," I whispered.

This man actually gasped as he squeezed my body so tightly, I was sure I'd be sore later. "I love you too damn much, King. *Too damn much.* The negotiating was fucked up and I know it, but I would've done anything to get us to where we are now. My bad on that shit, though. For real."

"I know. I believe you, and I'm glad we're together. I'm glad. I'm... happy."

"Me, too, baby. Me, too."

25

Memphis

The only appropriate soundtrack for the first few days after we returned from our honeymoon would be Soul II Soul's *Back to Life*. I touched base with Jerryn and Montana so we could finally go over what went wrong with the Mexico job and how we could avoid it in the future. Jerryn was upset that his source was late with the info about the senator's partners, and Montana apologized for not seeing it coming, although that really wasn't her job. With that handled, I arranged for my laundry service to pick up my clothes and gave Bo's chef a tour of my kitchen. I also called and checked in with my family. Additionally, I spent hours arguing with Bo about a bodyguard he'd hired for me.

For me!

I didn't need a damn bodyguard! I was a whole-ass killer!

Two weeks after we'd returned home, we still hadn't reached an agreement on it. So, when he came to me, eyes serious and determined, I just knew we were about to resume the argument.

"Bo, I don't give a fuck what you say—" I began.

He dropped onto the sofa next to me and sighed as he interrupted me. "I'm not trying to argue about that anymore. I need to show you something."

"What?" I snapped.

"You gotta be mean all the time? Damn!"

"Gotta keep my guard up because you might be showing me a picture of your side chick or something." I was kind of kidding and kind of serious at the same time. Yeah, he got on my nerves, but he was only allowed to annoy me, no one else.

"I'm not even entertaining that dumb shit. Let me see your hand."

I frowned as I held my hand out to him and watched him turn it so that the palm was facing the ceiling. In it, he placed a key and what I recognized to be an external hard drive device.

My eyes rushed from my hand to his face. "What is this?"

"The keys to the kingdom. You're my wife, my partner. No more working in the field for you. You're gonna run this shit with me."

26

Memphis

Receiving the keys to the kingdom, The Agency, involved a field trip to a warehouse found on the outskirts of town. It was off an access road and hidden behind miles of trees. The driveway consisted of barely visible ruts in the overgrown grass and weeds, but the façade looked shiny and new, metal and steel bearing a severe contrast to the rustic landscape surrounding it. He pulled to a stop in front of the heavy-looking stark white metal door.

His usually unseen security pulled in right behind us. I supposed it was impossible to be stealth out here.

Bo retrieved his cell from the center console of his car, gripping it in his hand as he began to speak. "I'm sorry about what happened... before. I know I've already apologized, but I don't think I can apologize enough," he said, his eyes focused out the windshield.

"Then look at me and say it," I challenged.

He chuckled as his eyes met mine. "So fucking mean..."

"And you love it."

"I do." He leaned in and kissed me, adding, "I'm sorry. I wish none of it happened."

"It isn't all on you. There were others involved."

He nodded. "I know."

We sat there, eyes locked on one another for long minutes before another vehicle arrived, and out of it, stepped Bo's mother.

Fuck.

27

Memphis

Then…

I was uncharacteristically nervous. Usually, nothing got to me, but meeting this woman knowing how much Bo revered her had me more than a little shaken up. I kept my cool, though.

"You ready?" Bo asked as he slowly drove through the gate.

I nodded, my eyes on the massive house before me. It looked like it belonged in a soap opera or something. Huge, Tudor-style, rich.

"Yeah," I responded verbally. "You said she knows I work for the company, right?"

"Yep. She knows everything about the company. She's like a silent president or something, although I actually run things."

"So...she doesn't think this thing between us is...inappropriate? You being my boss and all?"

He shrugged. "I wouldn't give a fuck either way. She don't run me. She don't run you, either."

I didn't have a response for that.

Once he parked in the curved driveway, he reached over to grasp my hand and squeeze it. "I just want you to meet her. I ain't looking for her approval. I'ma grown ass man. Ain't nobody coming between us, Miss King."

I rolled my eyes.

In quick succession, he opened my door and led me up the wide steps through the unlocked front door. I thought that was weird until I saw the huge and obviously armed man standing in the foyer.

"Moody! You musta seen me coming and unlocked the door for me. Good looking out, man," Bo said to the giant.

In return, the assumed bodyguard or whatever nodded at him and eyed me. Then, we were in the posh living room where even more eyes found me—an older lady's, my former crush's, and a really pretty younger lady's.

Before Bo could utter a word, my former crush hopped up and shouted, "I knew it! I told you, Ma! He took her from me!"

Took me? I mean, yes, I liked him, but he was making me sound like a damn Matchbox car or something, a collector's item.

"Zaccai," Bo said, sounding bored, "how the fuck can I take something that was never yours?"

"Fuck you!" Zaccai bit out.

"And what is this? An ambush?" Bo asked, his eyes on his mother now.

"I could ask you the same thing, son," she said. She had a slight accent that I couldn't quite place.

"No, you invited me to dinner. Isn't it customary to bring a date? I didn't know you were inviting someone. Anyway, Ma, this is the beautiful Memphis King. Baby, this is my mother, Viktoria Pierce. You know my brother, Zaccai, and this is Layla Morton, a family friend."

I nodded and smiled. "Nice to meet you all."

"My God," the matriarch snorted. "Memphis, is it? Dear, Layla is betrothed to Bo. I don't know why he would bring you to meet me knowing you have no place in his future."

I snapped my head around to look at Bo. "Oh?" I said, my voice even, although my young heart was breaking.

"Nah, I ain't betrothed to nobody unless I say I am," Bo protested.

"And from what I've heard, you can't have children? Now, how is that going to work?" his mother directed to me.

My head swiveled around to face her. "How is that your business?" I could feel Bo's eyes on me, sense his pride.

"My son is my business," she advised me.

"I'm a grown ass man!" Bo shouted.

"A man with obligations," she countered.

There was a stare-down between mother and son before Bo damn near yanked me out of the house muttering, "Fuck this."

Then...

THE RIDE back to her place was silent until she said, "Does Layla live with you?"

I frowned. "Hell naw! You've been to my place. You know I live alone."

"Yeah, but you're always at my place. We rarely go to yours."

"Because I *like* your place."

"Hmm..."

"Come on, King. You don't seriously think I'm going to marry her. I'm always with you. I love *you*!"

"Your mom believes it vehemently."

"She *wants* it vehemently. She don't get to choose for me."

"You told her about my hysterectomy?"

"Of course I didn't. She has the same resources as I do. It would be easy for her to find out."

"Hmm..."

"King—"

"When we get to my place, don't come inside."

My fucking heart stopped. "What? What do you mean?"

"I mean, I need time to think about all this."

Shaking my head, I slapped the steering wheel. "No!"

"No? The fuck you mean no?"

"My bad, I meant to say *hell* no. You don't need to think about shit!"

"Bo, have you lost your mind?"

"Not yet, but I will if you try to shut me out."

"I need to think."

"No the-fuck you don't."

A millisecond after I parked in her parking lot, she hopped out of my car and I hopped out right behind her ass, pacing her all the way to her apartment and catching the door before she could slam it in my face.

"Bo, get the fuck out of here!" she hissed.

My head pounded in tandem with my heart as I clutched her

arms and pulled her into a kiss, her resistance quickly waning until she shoved my chest.

"You really are betrothed to her. I can see it in your eyes, hear it in your voice. You don't want to be, but you are. Why didn't you just tell me? Why didn't you leave me alone?" Her voice was so calm and steady; the shit was almost eerie. She was shutting down on me, closing me out.

"Because I don't want her. I want you. I *need* you." I sounded so fucking weak.

We stared at each other, chests heaving. When she rammed her mouth into mine, I felt my sanity falter. I was confused as hell, but that wasn't her fault. Shit was completely fucked up.

When she ended the kiss, I actually whimpered until I watched her snatch her dress over her head and kick her shoes off. Her panties and bra hit the floor, and I kept my eyes glued to her as she moved to bend over the sofa.

With my dick as hard as reinforced titanium, I rushed to her, dropping my pants and underwear. I plowed into her so fast and hard that I almost fell.

"Fuck," I grunted as I stroked and stroked, her pussy pulling me in deeper and deeper. I felt desperate, so damn desperate. I couldn't control my hands as they roamed her ass and back. I couldn't control the words erupting from my mouth as I begged her to stay with me, to be mine. My whole body felt like a sacrifice to her. I just needed her to feel and know that she was all I wanted. She was my heart, my fucking first love. I just...I needed her so badly.

As her walls shook around my dick, she began to sob, and I'll be damned if a tear or two didn't pop up on my face as my nuts exploded and my hips stammered to a ragged halt.

Memphis

Then...

WE FUCKED over and over again that night—frenetic couplings that burned hot, charged with frustration and angst and uncertainty. When we finally fell into a spent and much needed sleep, it was early the next morning. So, it made sense that neither of us saw what was coming.

What awakened me was the sensation of cold steel against my temple. What awakened Bo, was my yelp. A small crowd had gathered in my bedroom with two of them holding guns to our heads. The gunmen were unknown to me, but the person standing at the foot of my bed was familiar—Viktoria Pierce.

"You're a steely one, aren't you?" she said, amusement on her face as she looked at me. "If not for that little sound you made, I'd think your feathers weren't a bit ruffled."

"What the fuck are y'all doing here? Who are these niggas? The hell?" Bo said groggily.

"The accent. Where are you from?" I asked his mother.

"You're astute, too. Barbados. The accent has faded, but it's still there."

I nodded. "Is the island full of evil bitches, or is it just you?"

She laughed heartily as the stranger pushed the muzzle of his gun into my flesh.

"Look, just take the damn gun off her. You wanna play this shit with me? Fine. Leave her out of it." Bo wasn't the least bit afraid. He was boiling hot, though.

So was I.

"And forfeit my leverage?" She sucked her teeth. "What did I tell you? Evah pig got a Saturday, my Bo. Yuh don't listen. Now, I have to kill this girl so you'll understand."

I frowned. "Kill me? For what? You just complimented my intelligence, my observation skills. I'm an asset to your company."

"You are, but you are also a distraction for my son. I can't have that."

"You kill her, and you better kill me, too, because I won't stop until I fuck everything you ever loved up!" Bo declared, and I could tell he meant it.

My assigned shooter moved his gun to Bo's head, and I took the opportunity to leave the bed, butt ass naked and all.

"Got damn!" one of the men mumbled, his gaze on my ass.

I rolled my eyes as I turned to look at Bo who took the ass watcher's lapse in focus to grab his gun. Next, he leaped out of bed, his naked body making mine weep as he held the gun to the newly unarmed man's head.

"Ma, y'all better leave before I kill all y'all. I'm fucking deadass serious," Bo growled.

I moved to my dresser, pulling out a t-shirt and dropping it over my head before turning to watch the rest of the saga play out. Was I shook from waking up to a gun trained on me? Absolutely. I was a killer, but I was also a damn human being. More than anything, I was pissed at the invasion of my domain and the fucking blatant disrespect that was being displayed.

Oh, I was SEETHING.

"I have guns, too. Please leave. *Now*," I said bluntly.

Bo looked at me with pure adoration in his eyes.

"We'll leave, but do we have an understanding now?" his mother directed at me.

"Didn't your man just get killed? Shouldn't you be in mourning instead of over here fucking with me?" I countered.

Something flashed in her eyes before she gave me a weird ass smile. Nodding at her companions, she said, "I think our work here is done. Let's go."

The intruders filed out of my bedroom, the front door soon closing behind them.

I moved back to my dresser, finding a pair of panties in the drawer and pulling them on, although my pussy was a sticky mess from the previous night's festivities. Then I stood and stared into the drawer, trying to process what had just happened. Bo's familiar aura surrounded me as he pressed his body to the back of mine, and I shook my head.

"Bo..." I sighed.

His arms encircled my waist as his lips met the side of my neck, and I closed my eyes.

"Tell me what I can do to make you stay with me. We can get married today. Whatever you want," he offered.

"I'm still getting over my mother's death. I'm adjusting to a new job that I love, I'm..."

"Please, baby. *Please*. I can fix this. Just...just let me."

Against my better judgement and completely engulfed in this man's love, I said, "Okay."

28

Then...

I stood in my mother's living room, so fucking angry I could burn her motherfucking house to the ground. I loved my mother despite the fact that I knew she could be ruthless and downright evil in the pursuit of reaching a desired end. I knew she loved me and Zaccai and our father, however toxic and twisted that love might've been, but for her to bust into Memphis's place and threaten her life? She'd taken shit miles past too far.

Seated on the sofa as I stood before her, my mother crossed her legs and pursed her lips as she played with the strand of pearls around her neck. Her appearance was neat, well put together, and expensive, as usual.

"You're angry. Surely you know *your* life was never in danger," she said, her affect flat.

"You threatened to kill my woman! That's the same as threatening me!" I thundered.

She tilted her head to the side, recognition appearing in her small eyes. "Oh...you're in love." Sucking her teeth, she shook her head. "And I suppose she loves you, too?"

"She does."

My mother sighed and clicked her tongue. "That's a shame."

I shook my head, my fists clenched at my sides. "Nah, what's a shame is you thinking you can make decisions for me. I'm fucking grown!"

"Your father made a deal—"

"Fuck the deal! We got a company full of killers who can take care of Layla's father. Hell, I'll do it!"

"You will not! No harm will come to him!"

I frowned. "Why? Why not? I mean, *fuck him.* I didn't make the damn deal with him, and the man who did is dead."

Her eyes narrowed. "I noticed this Memphis girl doesn't have security. Strange, with her father being a blues legend, but also fortu-itous for me. It would be nothing to get rid of her. You can't be with her all the time. For instance, right now, she's home all alone...isn't she?"

I could feel my pulse banging in my temple. "Is that a fucking threat?"

"No..." she sang, tapping on her phone—a Japanese model most Americans didn't even have access to yet—and holding it up so that the screen was facing me. It was a grainy photo of Memphis sitting on her sofa. "It's a promise. This picture was taken by one of our company's killers, as you put it. He's just waiting for me to give him the go ahead. He's a great distance shooter."

"A sniper? Are you fucking serious?"

"I am. I'm very serious, son. I'll have her entire family eliminated."

At that moment, any love I held for my mother completely dissipated.

Then...

I HADN'T SEEN him all day and couldn't wait to be in his arms again. I knew he planned to meet with his mother. I also knew he was furious with her. I hoped their conversation wasn't too explosive, but I was sure of one thing: he wasn't letting me go for anyone. He loved me. That was doubtless.

I'd actually fallen asleep on my sofa when he finally arrived. He gently shook me awake and sat down beside me before pulling me into his arms. I damn near purred as I leaned into him, reaching up to kiss his neck. Before I could blink, we were both naked and he was between my legs, his fingers strumming my clit as he slid in and out of me. The living room was dark, so I couldn't see his face, but I could feel him. I could feel his ragged breaths against my lips as he lowered his head to kiss me. I could feel his dick stretching me, his generous girth repeatedly grazing my spot, his fingers rubbing my sensitive bud. My nose was full of the aroma of our joined bodies, and my ears rang from my own shrieks and moans. In no time, I felt that familiar orgasmic hysteria, the frenetic energy that gave me the most intense buzz, and in the aftermath, all my fuzzy brain could conjure was a singular thought: *I will never love another man the way I love Bo Pierce.*

His climax seemed to damn near incapacitate him as he grunted and whimpered before collapsing to the floor beside the couch. On automatic, I joined him, straddling him while kissing his lips and neck and chest.

I was sliding down to clean up the mess my pussy had made of his dick—with my mouth—when he said, "I got married today."

I stopped, face to face with his limp shaft, my brows furrowed. "What?" Surely, I was hearing things.

"I got married today...to Layla Morton."

I sat on my knees between his legs, my mind struggling to process his words.

"My pop made a deal with hers. It was part of this street war truce from back in the day when they were in Chicago. Laythen Morton only has one child, a daughter. My pop promised one of his sons would marry her and take care of her. He chose me," he continued.

I moved backward, putting space between us.

"I never intended to marry her. I don't have nothing against her, but if I was gonna get married, I planned to choose my own wife. Then you came along and robbed me of my heart and...I didn't wanna do it. I *had* to."

Now I was on my feet, my hands shaking. "You...had to?"

"Yeah, my mom ain't gonna let up, and as pissed as I am about it, I can't exactly fuck my mom up. You know? So, I did it, but nothing has to change between us. Plus, I ain't gotta stay married forever. Give me a little time. Just hold on."

"Nothing has to ch—get up."

"Yeah, we can still be us. I still love y—"

"Nigga, get the fuck UP! Get your ass up and get out of here! Now!"

I couldn't see him, but I knew when he got to his feet because almost instantly, I could feel his body heat near mine. When his hand met my arm, I slapped it away.

"Don't touch me! Don't you ever touch me again. You just forfeited that privilege."

"King—"

"And you had the nerve to fuck me on your wedding night?!"

"Wasn't a wedding. Not really. We got married in my mother's living room."

My response to that bit of information was to slap the shit out of him. "Leave! I don't ever want to see you again!"

"But you work for me."

"I work for The Agency. I was never supposed to meet you in the first place. Give me another point of contact, or I'll quit."

"Baby—"

"I mean it!"

His response was to silently get dressed and leave, but not before offering me a somber, "I really do love you."

29

Memphis

Now...

I hated this woman, and I was sure it showed, not that it was a fact she was unaware of anyway. Hell, the feeling was most certainly mutual. She hadn't arrived alone but with Zaccai, Moody, and Layla in tow. Bo's son, Tavares, had accompanied her as well. I knew him because I'd been a bit of a stalker of Bo for many years after he obliterated my heart. I knew exactly when Tavares had arrived.

After his three security guys checked the building, Bo led me inside and let the door slam just as his family approached it, flipping on a light switch and illuminating the massive, hollow structure he called a compound. There was a long glass table with black chairs in the middle of the space and little else. He pulled a chair out for me and dropped into one next to it. Together, we watched in silence as the others filed in. One thing about the Pierce matriarch was that she was always going to put that shit on. The gray pantsuit she wore paired with lime green pumps was gorgeous and so was she. She was a beautiful gray-haired bitch who looked much younger than her age. Layla was her mini me as far as style, and she was pretty, too—light skin, freckles, little pixie nose, doe eyes. I wasn't sure how she survived being married to Bo.

"You bringing your woman to company meetings now?" Zaccai asked Bo. For some reason, he was on crutches and had a cast on one of his legs and a boot on the opposite foot. He must've fallen and hurt the other leg or something after Bo shot him.

Damn.

"Why not? You brought yours, didn't you?" Bo shot back.

Mother Pierce dropped into a chair across from us and flapped her hand. "Not this again. You didn't even want Layla. You don't care about her seeking comfort with your brother, do you?"

What the fuck?

How did I not already know this? Probably because I never bothered to stalk Zaccai's lame ass, but still, *wow*.

"Oh, I don't give even half a shit who she fucks. She had to get it from somewhere because she damn sure wasn't getting it from me."

Zaccai shook his head. "So, you tryna pretend you ain't fuck your wife for *her* benefit?" Zaccai asked, nodding toward me. "We ain't stupid, Bo."

"No. I *did* fuck her from time to time out of duty," Bo said, shrugging "She enjoyed it."

That shit made my skin crawl, although I never believed he *didn't* fuck her.

"Turned out, I wasn't her first choice, either. She had a man before and during our marriage. Not exactly sure why she decided to fuck with you when she had other options," Bo replied. "As a matter of fact, me and Layla were friends until...well, I won't get into that."

"Nah, go ahead and say it," Tavares spoke up. He was a handsome young man with a nasty ass attitude from what I could tell.

"The only thing I gotta say to you, *son*, is that I should've left your ass on the street where I found you," Bo admitted.

Tavares shrugged. "I always knew I was a temporary project for you. You know, take the troubled teenager off the street, buy him shit, clean him up, and expect him to worship you. That's what you did, ain't it?"

Bo sighed, tapping his finger on the table. "No, I actually cared about you. Didn't know you were as fucked up as you ended up being. I also didn't know Layla was nasty enough to fuck you, but at least she waited until you were nineteen."

What?!

"Kiss my ass, Bo. At least I didn't sit around pining for a mediocre bitch for decades," Layla said.

"Mediocre? Mediocre?" I uttered, my hand moving toward the gun nestled in my ankle holster beneath my slacks.

"Don't bother, baby. I'll kill her," Bo said, resting a hand on my arm.

"Enough! What are you going to do? Shoot her like you did your brother twice? Shoot up this building like you did my house?" his mother asked with a scowl on her perfectly made-up face.

He did what?!

"It was only the foyer," Bo countered.

"Bo, why is she here?" the matriarch asked, her displeased eyes on me now.

Fucking mega bitch.

Bo grasped my hand, squeezing it. "I called this meeting on

neutral ground to let you all know Memphis and I are married now, and she will join me in running The Agency."

Zaccai shrieked, "What?! She ain't even blood! I should be running this shit! Not her ho' ass!"

Bo hopped up and was around the table in what felt like a literal flash, his gun pressed to the side of Zaccai's head.

"I told you to keep your mouth off her, didn't I? The first two bullets didn't get my point across?" Bo bit out.

Zaccai lifted his hands. "Okay, okay! My bad, man. I'm just...I'm shocked."

"Anybody else got some shit to say about her? Please speak up but know that she's the only one in here who's safe from death," Bo announced.

"All I have to say is...welcome to the family, Memphis," his mother offered.

"Um...thanks?" I replied.

I HAD my chef prepare a bunch of meals and bring them to Memphis's high-rise instead of him cooking them here. Now that she was my wife, I didn't want to share space with anyone but her. We were sitting at her modern-looking glass dining room table, eating blackened chicken with asparagus when she finally broke a silence she'd settled into when we left The Agency's compound earlier.

"Your mother threatened to kill me. That's why you married that woman. You made some kind of deal with your mother to keep me safe," she stated, her voice bearing the certainty of a new revelation.

I stopped mid-chew and looked up at her to find her pretty eyes on me. Swallowing my food, I nodded and confirmed, "Yes."

"That's why you've been keeping tabs on me all these years, having me followed and I didn't even know it."

"It is. You've had the best security money can buy."

"So...you made the deal but didn't trust her to keep up her end of it?"

"Correct. I..." Falling against the back of my chair, I shook my head. "I adored my mother for a long time despite her overbearing personality, but the thing with me and you, the way she acted, it opened my eyes to a lot of shit about her I'd been blind to."

"Like what?"

I bit my bottom lip and stared down at the table. This was some uncomfortable shit, but I owed so much to Memphis, especially the truth. "She doesn't like me. Never has."

"You think that why? Because she fucked us up or because she gave you that horrific name?"

I chuckled. "Both, and other things. You know me and Zaccai don't have the same father, right?"

"You don't?!" Her voice had risen about three octaves.

"We don't. My dad raised him as his own, but she was already pregnant with him when they met. She always coddled Zaccai, protected him. When my pop passed, she threw me into running The Agency, hoping I'd fail. She actually said that shit. She said she knew my dad would want his *real* son to run things, so she was gonna let me fuck up and then give it to Zaccai. Now, she tries to act like she chose me because she knew I'd succeed."

"Bo..."

"She pushed me into that marriage, and I had to leverage some shit to get out of it."

"Leverage what?"

"I don't want to talk about that."

"Okay."

"Anyway, I refused to give her a biological grandchild. Pulled Tavares off the streets instead. That kinda backfired, though. She loves his ass more than I do."

"He hurt you. I'm sorry about that."

I shrugged. "I ain't no angel, either. It's all part of the game."

"Yeah."

"I got you back. That's all that matters. It's all I ever wanted."

She stared at me for a moment before standing and walking around the table to me.

"Scoot back," she ordered, and like the obedient pet I'd become for her, I did.

She slipped into my lap, wrapping her arms around me, the scent of her favorite parfum—Aqua Universalis—permeating my nose. Her lips met mine in a long, lingering, dick-hardening kiss, and when she pulled back, a look of horror covered her face. My eyes widened as I reached up to wipe the blood first from her face and then mine. Her nose was bleeding.

"Baby, what the fuc—"

She hopped up and raced out of the dining room before I could finish my statement. I followed her and was met with her slamming and locking the bathroom door.

"Memphis, let me in!" I shouted. "What the fuck is going on with you?!"

"Go away!" she growled.

"Hell no! You're my fucking wife. Something is wrong, and it's scaring the shit out of me! Don't make me kick this door in!"

The lock on the door clicked, and I yanked it open to find her sitting on the toilet holding a towel to her nose, her eyes shimmering with tears. She looked so vulnerable, a word I'd only associated with her one other time in all the years I'd loved her, the morning we woke up with guns to our heads. Truthfully, seeing her like that was really what made me let her go, even though it tore my heart out the fucking frame.

Kneeling before her, I reached up and moved the towel. "Looks like it stopped."

She nodded, a single tear escaping her eye. "Bo, I'm scared. I'm really scared. I keep feeling dizzy, and now this..."

"Dizzy? Memphis..." Holding her soft face in my hands, I admitted, "I'm scared, too, but we'll get you to a doctor and see what's going on."

She shook her head. "I don't trust doctors. You know that."

"I get that, but we don't have a choice."

"Maybe it's nothing. Maybe it'll just go away."

"Let the doctor tell you that."

"I'm not—"

"Memphis, I'm not trying to be insensitive, but I ain't tryna hear that shit. I just got you back, and I don't want nothing cutting my time with you short. I don't give a fuck if I have to sedate your ass, tie you to the bed, and force a doctor to come here, you getting checked thefuck out!"

She lifted her head, fixing her wet eyes on mine. "A female doctor, then."

"Done."

THIS SHIT HURT—WATCHING the baddest woman I'd ever known look so afraid, so...defeated as she listened to the doctor go over her lab results. I was in fucking shambles. If whatever was going on was going to take her away from me, I was going to fucking kill everyone I knew and a few people I didn't know. I was going to become a prolific mass assassin. Wait, I was already that.

"The values I'm most concerned about are your red blood cell count, hemoglobin, and hematocrit. They're all out of range, elevated," the doctor was saying. "You say you're not a smoker, right?"

"Correct. Why?" Memphis replied, her eyebrows in a tangle.

"Well, smoking can effect these values, but that's obviously not the case in this instance."

"Okay...what's going on, then? What's wrong with me?"

"You will need to undergo further testing for confirmation, but these test results coupled with the symptoms you've been experiencing—dizziness, light-headedness, nose bleeds, headaches, blurred vision..."

I didn't even know half this shit was happening! My got damn heart was breaking knowing she was dealing with this alone. She hadn't even told her family.

"...I believe we're dealing with Polycythemia Vera," the doctor finished.

"W-what is that?" Memphis stammered.

"It's a blood disease."

Memphis blinked a few times before saying, "Okay. How do we treat it? Is it curable?"

The doctor nodded, giving Memphis a reassuring smile. "It's *very* treatable, but first, I need to refer you to a colleague of mine. Dr. Sandra Sutton. She's an excellent oncologist. She'll want to do some genetic testing—"

"An oncologist? I have...this blood disease is-is cancer?"

"Yes."

30

She requested that we go to my house, so that's where I took her. My wife was not an overly emotional person except for when it came to anger. There were no tears, just silence. Silence as we left the doctor's office, silence on the ride through the city to my home in the suburbs, silence when I opened the passenger door for her and led her into the house. Silence as I followed her up the stairs and watched her climb into bed. Her energy in that moment was so foreign to me that it alarmed me. My wife, my badass soulmate was...broken. I didn't have a clue what to do or say. I just stood at the foot of the bed for a few minutes before climbing in beside her, and before I could touch her, she scooted toward me, pressing her body to mine. My dick was hard in picoseconds, as was the usual when any part of my body made contact with hers, but I told myself that fucking wasn't appropriate at the present time.

"I thought I was being so smart. I thought I was dodging the cancer bullet by getting a hysterectomy," she said into my chest, her voice soft and audibly vulnerable. "Joke's on me. Then again, I couldn't expect to kill people for decades with no repercussions."

Resting my chin on her head, I asked, "That's what you think this is? Karma?"

"What else could it be?"

"Life. Genetics. Can't run from either, and if we wanna talk punishment for wrongdoing, I'm more likely the target for this shit."

"How, when I'm the one with blood cancer?"

"Don't you know by now that the only way anyone or any entity, deity, *anything* can hurt me is by hurting you? Nobody, and I mean *nobody else* matters to me. You are the reason I'm still alive. You're the reason I fucking breathe. You and you alone."

I felt her shake her head before she said, "You loved your father. You love your mother. I think you still love your brother and your son. You cared about your ex-wife at some point because you said you were friends."

"My family...that shit is complicated."

"So complicated that you'd shoot your brother and your mom's house? I didn't forget that shit. Just wasn't sure I wanted to know the reason."

"First of all, it wasn't her entire house. It was the foyer. Second, you know the reason."

"Bo, I love you, but ain't no way I'd shoot any of my family members or their property over you."

"That's fair, especially since none of your family has done the evil, swamp rat shit mine has. Threatening you, disrespecting you, dismissing what we shared when the shit was and still is the realest thing I've ever experienced."

"Okay, I see your point."

"Baby?"

"Yeah?"

"It's okay to be scared. It's okay to be worried. This is some serious shit going on with your health."

"I don't want to be scared or worried. I don't know how to really exist in those emotions. All I know to do is fight."

"Then let's fight this thing. Let's fight it together."

THE ONCOLOGIST, Dr. Johnson, tested my blood again, confirming that my damn blood cells were fucked up. Then she explained the genetic testing, which involved them sticking a needle in my hip bone to do a bone marrow biopsy. She said I could be awake with a local anesthetic, or they could knock me out. She also said there would probably still be some pain either way. I told her they'd better knock me out if they didn't want me to involuntarily fuck up the person with the needle.

Bo co-signed with, "On God, she will."

Now, I was sitting in her office listening to her tell me that I'd tested positive for a mutation or change in the *PAK2* gene, something found in ninety-five percent of Polycythemia Vera patients.

"So...I definitely have cancer," I stated, my head feeling tight as Bo squeezed my hand. A glance over at him beside me told me he was three seconds from kicking the doctor's ass merely for reporting the findings. This was messing him all the way up.

"Yes, but I want you to frame this correctly. It is a type of cancer in that it involves uncontrolled cell production, which is the very definition of cancer. In your case, it's your red blood cells. This overproduction of cells can lead to many problems if left untreated, including stroke, blood clots, serious, serious issues. What makes it stand apart from other forms of cancer is its treatability. With proper treatment, you can live a normal life for decades to come."

"Really?" Bo peeped.

Pun intended.

"Absolutely," the doctor assured him.

"Is the treatment painful? Is it going to mess me up like chemo or something?" I questioned.

"Chemo isn't usually a route we take. For you, we're going to start with a daily dose of aspirin to thin the blood and some blood draws to help lower your hematocrit," Dr. Johnson shared.

"Th-that's it?" I squeaked.

"Well, you'll also need to modify your diet, avoid salt, exercise, avoid low oxygen environments—no mountain climbing or skiing. Maintain good skin care. You'll need to avoid extreme temperatures when you can. Really bundle up during wintry weather. Avoid hot tubs—"

"Aye, can you write all that shit down? I ain't gonna remember all this," Bo inquired.

The poor doctor's eyes widened at the gruffness in his voice, but she still managed to reply with, "Yes, of course. We'll be sending you all home with a multitude of information."

Bo squeezed my hand, and with a bright smile, told me, "We got this, baby. We can do this."

Returning his smile, I agreed, "Yeah, we can."

31

Memphis

"I s no one going to say anything?" I asked as my eyes roamed the room. My words were met with sustained heavy silence.

Finally, Umber spoke up. "We don't know what to say. Cancer? I just..." she shook her head, standing from the kitchen table.

"Umber, did you not hear everything I said? It's treatable and not necessarily terminal."

She nodded but didn't respond verbally.

"We *did* hear that. It's just that...this is scary, Mem," Lilith murmured.

I nodded. "It is, but this...it's not like with Mama. We caught it early, and it's more chronic than terminal. Treatment is simple, and the main thing is me actually taking care of myself."

Again, Bo was sitting right beside me, his hand engulfing mine, his eyes glued to me. This man was proving to be my rock for real.

Wow.

My eyes wandered over to my father whose attention didn't seem to be focused on anything or anyone. "Daddy, you okay?" I inquired.

Flanked by his two wives, he shifted his eyes to me as he sighed. "No, I ain't. I ain't nowhere near okay, but I know you. You're smart and tough. Always been a fighter. You sound confident, so I can't do nothing but trust you." Looking at Bo, he added, "She's your wife. She might be strong, but you better have her back. I don't play about my girls."

I held my breath, hoping I wasn't going to have to fuck my husband up for talking crazy to my daddy.

"Sir, I have loved your daughter since the day I met her many years ago. She's my heart, my everything. I will lay down my life for her in a second. Whatever she needs, I got it," Bo said.

Daddy nodded, and when my eyes found my brother-in-law, Ray, I saw something rare in his—respect, and I instinctually knew it was for Bo.

IN THE DARKNESS of our suburban bedroom, I buried my face in his chest and inhaled deeply. He always smelled like an intoxicating combination of bergamot, musk, and utter audacity with an overflow of confidence.

"What's on your mind, baby?" he asked, his deep voice oozing over me like warm chocolate.

Lifting my head, I kissed his neck. "Wondering when you're going to tell your family about my illness."

He chuckled. "Never. They don't need to know. Ain't their business."

"O...kay."

"Baby, Zaccai is a coward who hates me because I'm not one. Tavares is a fucked-up kid who can't get past his trauma to see that I truly cared about him and tried to take care of him. I even sent him to therapy, and he jumped on the damn therapist. Layla is just fucking trifling and hangs on to my mother for money. And my mother?" He paused. "My mother had my father killed, and she knows I know it."

32

"**W**hat?!" Memphis shrieked, inching out of my arms and turning on a lamp. "How do you know this?!"

I glued my eyes to the ceiling. "It never made sense to me that someone could get the jump on him like that."

"Same. He was a damn martial arts master. He always preached hyper vigilance. No way someone surprised him."

"Right, and there were cameras outside and inside the dojo. If someone was outside, he knew."

"Did anyone check the cameras?"

"Of course. They'd been disabled."

"Oh, shit! Then it had to be an inside job."

"Exactly. I started doing some research a couple years after I married Layla because I just couldn't move on. I needed to figure out what the fuck happened. I ran across some other security footage in the city, even traffic cams. Hell, I got my computer guy to check out Tennessee airport footage, highway convenience store footage, Romey hotel footage. Finally found the smoking gun at a convenience store outside of Romey in the form of Layla's father."

"Wait, you think he did it? You think he killed your father?"

"I *know* he did. He *told* me he did."

"Huh? Oh, shit, you killed him, didn't you? You killed your damn father-in-law."

"Crazy thing is, I didn't. I damn sure would've, but I didn't have to. I went to his place out in the country, about twenty miles west of Parkton, a huge-ass mansion. Dude was at death's door by then, some kind of rare lung disease. He was on oxygen, could barely breathe. Of course, I knew all that, but I rarely visited him, so I didn't realize how bad off he was, and Layla didn't really talk to me about it. I'm not sure where Layla was that day, probably with her man, but anyway, dude told me he was broke and that that big ass house was in foreclosure. He said he made a deal with my mom because his money was drying up. He'd kill my dad, and she'd make sure Layla was taken care of and give him some money that he quickly blew through."

"That's why she was so adamant about you marrying her."

"Yeah, and that's why she still takes care of Layla, albeit with money from my fucking company, a company my father built with her help. Anyway, the motherfucker died right after he confessed. I watched him take his last breath before I left. Layla discovered his body the next day."

"Damn."

"Right."

Memphis was quiet for a moment before she asked, "How does your mother know that you know she set your father up?"

"I told her when I was ready to divorce Layla."

"Oh, you had to get *ready* to divorce her?"

"Actually, I had to get ready to bring it to my mom. Shit was hard to accept. Anyway, I reiterated the fact that I knew what she did when I found a way to get you back in my life—"

"You mean, when you decided to blackmail me?"

"Call it what you want, but the shit worked out."

"Whatever."

"As I was saying, I informed her of our impending reconciliation and told her to stay the fuck out of it and the fuck away from you or I would tear her shit down."

"What does that even mean?"

"Baby, I finance her life. I threatened to cut her ass off. I can't seem to bring myself to kill her. Hell, I only injured Zaccai."

"More than once."

I shrugged.

"Well...she's your mother. I can see killing her being hard."

"Her being my mother don't keep me from despising her ass, though."

"Oh, I totally understand that."

33

Memphis

"**D**amn, like...this is a lot to take in at once! You're firing us *and* you're sick?! The fuck?!" Montana said, her image on the computer screen clear. She was a pretty young lady with wild red hair and medium brown skin. Her wide eyes seemed distant as she spoke.

"Right. Shit, Raja. I don't know what to say," Jerryn added.

"There's nothing to say. I'm done working in the field, and I have a chronic disease that I'm managing," I restated.

"Yeah, I guess you marrying the boss should've prepared me for the change in career. That ain't even my main concern. It's the disease. You're too fucking mean to be sick," Jerryn observed, making me laugh.

"Well damn," I replied.

"Oh, I agree with him. Any disease should be scared of your ass. You might shoot it!" Montana declared.

"Uh, since the disease is in my body, I definitely won't be doing that," I assured her.

"Right, your gun only points outward," Jerryn said.

"Bingo!" I chimed.

"Well, if you ever need me, I'm here for you. Anything, anytime," Jerryn offered.

"Same here!" Montana trilled.

"I appreciate you both," I said, coming as close to tears as I ever had. I'd miss these two.

"Oнннннн, shit! Shit-damn-fuck! Bo! Bo! BO!" I screamed, absolutely delirious at that point. If this man couldn't eat a pussy, then pussy just couldn't be eaten at all. He was devouring me like I was a bowl of the finest, authentic New Orleans gumbo, and I wasn't even sure how I felt about it. I mean, I loved it, but I didn't have the brain capacity to eloquently articulate that, so I screamed, bit my bottom lip, and wriggled beneath him while I gripped his head. My legs trembled; my eyes rolled to the back of my head. The orgasm felt like it burst through my pelvis, destroying everything in its path, and then he was deep inside me.

"How in the fuck could you still feel so good. It's like we were never apart. I used to dream about being inside of you, and this is what my dreams felt like. Fucking euphoria," he rambled.

"I...feel...the same...but not reallyyyyy! I-I-I think all the hate I built up for you makes the d-d-dick better!"

"Mm-hmmm..." he hummed, repeating the sound over and over

again as his strokes grew harder and faster and deeper until we were both howling through our mutual release.

Minutes later, as we lay beside each other with our naked bodies damp with sweat, he asked, "I know I hurt you, but you get it now, right? That I didn't want us to be apart? That I didn't want to marry her?"

"I do. It just...you stayed married to her, raised a kid with her. I don't know...that part still hurts," she admitted.

"I was married to her for six years, yes. I barely touched her, was hardly ever in the same room with her, baby. She ain't help me raise shit, either. Tavares was fifteen when I adopted him. Wasn't too much raising left to do, and what little I tried to do didn't stick."

"She was pregnant. I know she lost the baby, but still, you got her pregnant."

"Nah, it wasn't mine. I ain't never fuck her raw."

"Ew."

"You need to hear this shit, and I'm telling you. Her side nigga, the one she had before we got hitched? It was his. Dude was a low-level drug dealer, so her dad didn't want her to marry him. Anyway, she didn't miscarry. Her dad made her abort it when he found out. Shortly after that, he died, and Layla started fucking Zaccai. She's still fucking him, far as I know."

"Damn."

"Yep."

"You were always fucking with me, though, playing all those psychological games and shit like contacting me with assignments, picking targets for me, telling me who to train. You hurt me, and then you wouldn't leave me alone!"

He chuckled, and I barked, "The fuck is funny?!"

"You! Your silly ass don't realize that was my way of taking care of you. I was making sure you made the easiest money doing the safest jobs. The contacting you myself part was selfish. I just wanted to interact with you, hear your voice. I missed you. Then I started missing you so bad that it actually hurt to contact you, so I stopped. I still picked the assignments that were presented to you, though."

"Oh."

"Uh-huh, so...you still hate me, baby?"

In response, I moved to straddle him, perching myself right on his dick, and felt when it began to rise. "What you think?"

He gazed up at me before grasping my face and pulling it down to his. "I think I fucking love you."

With my lips grazing his, I said, "I'm pretty sure I love you, too."

34

Memphis

"**N**igga, move! I'm tryna work out!" I fussed.

Bo was all up on my ass laughing as I bent over to pick up the dumbbells. "Oh, is that what you were doing? I thought that was a signal," he said, gripping my butt cheeks.

"A signal for what?"

"Fucking," he said, his voice deadpan.

"Bo, move! Shit!"

"Fine, mean ass, and speaking of asses, make sure you get some squats in. If you lose that booty, I'ma cry."

Rolling my eyes, I turned to see him leaning against the front of his treadmill. smiling at me. He converted his formal dining room into a gym long before I moved in, but I never bothered using it until I received my diagnosis. I always figured killing people was enough exercise for me.

"You look happy," I observed as I began doing bicep curls with the eight-pound weights.

"I am. Why you using them baby-ass weights?"

"Because I'm tired from the constant fucking your old ass has me doing."

His eyebrows flew up. "Old ass, huh?"

"Old as hell."

His smile widened. "You about three seconds from fifty yourself, ain't it?"

"So is my pussy."

"Yeah, it's aging like the finest of wines. Motherfucker is priceless."

"That's what I'm saying."

"Riiiight, so...my mother has invited us to dinner."

"Why? You stop her deposits or something? She wanna evaluate my performance as manager although I haven't really done anything?"

"First of all, she don't run *shit* at The Agency. Second, you're the fucking boss right along with me. Can't no-fucking-body evaluate you. Third, I thought we agreed you were going to focus on your health right now." His voice softened with the last sentence.

"We did. I just feel like I'm not pulling my weight around here."

"That pussy pulling *all* the weight."

I sighed, dropping the weights on the floor. "Why'd she invite us?"

He shrugged. "She told me some bullshit about it being a while since she's seen or talked to me, talking 'bout she misses me."

"You don't believe her?"

"Hell no! I don't trust shit that comes out of her mouth."

"So...we're not going?"

"Hell to-the motherfucking no!"

"I'm cool with that decision," I said with a shrug.

"Oh, I know you are. I'ma set up a call or something. Maybe a video chat, but I ain't giving her or nobody else in her household a chance to ambush me."

"You think they'd really do something like that? I know Tavares is a hot head, but he doesn't seem calculated enough to do anything."

"Yeah, but he's devoted to my mom. She spoils him because he's her only grandchild."

"Well, Zaccai is too weak."

"True. Hey, enough about my messed-up family. Now, what's your plan for keeping them thighs juicy? I'll cry if they get skinny."

I sighed again and shook my head.

"Damn, this is really...regular. Nothing like your high-rise place. You like living here?" Umber said, her eyes sweeping the living room.

"I do. It's a quiet neighborhood, and it ain't like I'm living here alone," I pointed out.

"Yeah, you definitely aren't," Lilith muttered.

I sighed. "What's on your mind, Lil?"

She shrugged, raking her fingers through her hair. "It's just that I barely get to talk to you anymore; you don't come to visit..."

"Oh, so you wanna act brand new? You gonna act like you didn't ghost the whole family when you first got with Ray?" I asked.

Her eyes widened. "I lost contact after I left Marlon. Ray just happened to come along around the same time," Lilith countered.

"Yeah, she was in mourning. Besides, we're used to you calling to check on us and stuff, big sis," Umber said. Her ass was actually pouting.

My mouth dropped open. "Really Danielle Boone? You're a virtual recluse out there in the woods! You don't fool with nobody!"

"Nobody but her dog," Lilith corrected me.

"That's why you're supposed to be checking on me!" Umber whined.

I stared at her and lifted a brow when a thought hit me. "Umby, are you...you feeling lonely because Lilith and I are both married now?"

Lilith gasped. "Oh! Are you, Umber?"

Our baby sister lifted one shoulder and dropped it. "I don't know. It's like, y'all have these self-contained lives now. Everything is shifting. I just want us to communicate more."

"Me, too," I said. "Look, I've had so much going on. New marriage. Trying to manage my health. It's a lot, but I'ma always love my family. *Always.*"

"Damn, my bad. How are you feeling? You look great," Umber said sheepishly.

"I feel good so far. Bo takes good care of me," I said, suppressing a smile.

"Oh, we can see that. He seems so...aggressive. I bet he's tearing you up in bed," Lilith said.

"I wasn't gonna say nothing, but..." Umber mumbled.

"I wouldn't be with him if he wasn't," I informed them. "Anyway, let's go in the kitchen and eat since I *did* invite y'all to have lunch with me. Bo's chef can cook his ass off."

"A chef? What did you say he does for a living?" Umber questioned.

"He's in corporate management."

"Hey, where is he?" Lilith queried.

"He's spending time with his mom today."

"When do we get to meet his family?" Umber asked.

"Never. I can't stand those motherfuckers," I declared.

"Well, damn. Uh, let me hit the bathroom you showed us before we eat," Umber said.

Lilith and I were in the kitchen when she moved close to me and whispered, "I still can't believe you married your boss."

I frowned, setting the plates I'd gathered on the island. "Lil, don't start."

"I'm just saying…"

"*Please* don't."

Just then, Umber returned yelling, "Let's eat!"

I BROKE WEAK, or maybe a more truthful way of looking at it was, she broke me down. She, being my mother. She kept calling, basically begging to see me, and shit, she was *my mother*. So, I finally agreed, taking one bodyguard with me and leaving the other two to watch over Memphis who swore they were sorcerers or something because she rarely saw them, even though they were always present. That was by design, of course. I didn't want her upset at me because she could take care of herself. I knew she could, but I needed the extra assurance. In truth, her security was for *my* peace of mind. She didn't need to know I'd bought the house across the street from my place for them to hole up in. She didn't need to know their names, either, although that information was at her fingertips. All she needed to do was be. I just needed her to be, and while being, to be with me. That was it.

I hated to leave her to meet with my mother, but I also didn't want to bring her with me and end up shooting my mom if she disrespected her. I still owed Zaccai another bullet for talking slick at that last meeting.

We met at The Bell Room, a café in The Village known for their tea cakes. I loved me some damn tea cakes.

I arrived a whole hour early, waited for my security to check everything out, and was told my mother was already there. I found her sitting in a corner booth nursing a cup of coffee.

Dropping onto the seat across from her, I asked, "Just you and Moody and the guys outside?" I nodded toward Moody sitting a few tables away from us, failing to blend in with the other patrons. Dude was too damn huge.

She smiled. "Yes. Always aware of your surroundings..."

"Mm-hmm, just like my father."

"If you're fishing for an apology, you won't get one. I did what I had to do to protect you and Zaccai."

I chuckled. "No, you did that for yourself. I'm sure of that."

She shrugged. "Partly. He was trying to cut me off. Believe me, he owed me."

I nodded. "Whatever you say."

She sighed, took a sip of her coffee, and fixed her eyes on me. "I didn't ask to meet you to argue. I want...I *need* a truce. I want to be a part of your life. I'm not getting any younger, and I just...you're my son. I love you."

I stared at her. I might have had a soft spot for the woman who raised me, but this was too far out of character to be believable.

She blew out a breath, reclining in her seat. "Bo, I'm serious. I know you're angry about how things panned out with Miss King in the past—"

"*Mrs.* Pierce," I corrected her.

This woman visibly flinched before rubbing the back of her neck. Her mouth opened, but no words were spoken.

"What has Memphis ever done to you?" I asked, my pulse thumping in my temple. "Our family swooped in when she was young and pulled her into our world. She has done her job better than anyone else at the company. She's intelligent and efficient. She has a good heart, and she still loves me despite what you did to us, what I *let* you do to us. What's your fucking problem?!" I somehow kept my volume low, but she couldn't have missed the venom in my voice.

Her gaze dropped to the table as she said, "To be honest, she reminds me of myself."

"So...you hate yourself?"

She smiled and shook her head, eyes still on the table. "No, I think I envy her. I envy that you love her so much. I could see it in you when you brought her to meet me for the first time. I knew you'd give her the world...and you did."

I frowned. "Ain't that how love is supposed to work?"

"In theory, yes. Didn't work out like that for me."

"So, all this time, it was jealousy...."

Finally, her eyes met mine again. "Yes. Your love for her endured all these years, and I realize you purposely didn't have children with Layla because of Memphis. I thank you for Tavares, though. He's a light."

"Tavares is an ungrateful ass."

"He's misunderstood."

"Like Zaccai, huh? You love to make excuses for sorry ass niggas."

"You're so much like your father; it's actually a little frightening. He was so no-nonsense."

I shrugged. "What's going on, Ma? Why are we here?"

She sighed, her gaze now out the window beside us. "I'm getting old. As I said, I want to be a part of your life."

I smiled. "Don't worry. I won't cut you off as long as you show my wife the respect she deserves. An apology would be nice, too."

"I'm not worried about money. I want my son. I love you."

Our eyes were locked, and though she looked and sounded sincere, my cold-ass heart couldn't accept it. She'd wreaked too much havoc in my life, upending my one real source of happiness—Memphis King.

So, all I did was grunt, "I'll think about it."

35

Memphis

"So, your sister lunch was a hit, huh?" Bo asked.

We were in my favorite position—naked, skin to skin with my face in his chest inhaling a scent I'd memorized decades ago, the fragrance of *him*.

"Yep. We decided to take turns hosting lunch every couple of weeks. Umber volunteered for the next one, but I'ma have to make an excuse to miss it. I ain't tryna eat some damn fried squirrel legs out in the middle of nowhere," I replied.

He chuckled. "Why you acting like she lives in a lean-to or a pop-up tent or something?"

"Close enough. It's a damn decommissioned fire lookout tower thing, or at least the cabin attached to it. She has a pre-law degree but decided not to go to law school, came home from college, worked a corporate job, saved her money, and bought her place. I don't know. I think between our mom's death and her first love ghosting her, she just said fuck it and decided to commune with nature, hunting and foraging for food."

"Damn. She still working the corporate job?"

"No, she owns her own hiking coordination company or something like that. It's called Trill Trailblazers. It keeps her bills paid."

"She leads the hikes or just plans them?"

"Both. She's hiked all over the country."

"Damn, she must be in top tier shape."

"Right."

"My mom is jealous of you," he said randomly.

"Huh? She told you that?"

"Yep. She says she always knew I'd give you the world, which was something my father never gave her."

"The world?"

"The Agency. It's always about The Agency with her."

"Didn't she help him create and run it?"

"Yeah, but once the money started rolling in, he kind of shut her out of the business, giving her limited access."

"I see. Why didn't she just take over when he was killed, then?"

"Why would she when she could let me do the work while she reaped the benefits?"

"Damn, you got a point there, Mr. Pierce."

MY EYES POPPED open to darkness and the harshness of Bo's whisper.

"You hear that?" he asked.

"Not sure, but something woke me up," I softly returned, reaching for my gun on the nightstand.

"I tried to check the cameras. They're all down. Security ain't answering my calls and them niggas right across the street, all three of them."

"Across the street? I knew it! The house with the gray door, right?"

"Yeah, but baby, focus. I'm tryna figure out what the fuck is going on."

The hair on my arms stood at attention as a realization hit me. "It's an ambush."

"Yeah."

In the darkness, I felt him leave the bed, and I hissed, "The fuck are you going? Ain't no telling who's outside this room. Close and lock the door."

"Damn, that's what the fuck I was about to do."

"You got your gun?"

"Memphis, you gotta chill. When do I *not* have a gun? The hell?"

"There you go with that Memphis shit again."

"You wanna address that right now? Really?"

"My bad," I whispered. "Wait!" I stood, navigating my way to him, my gun ready. "Okay, go," I said, my hand on his back.

"You literally got my back, huh?" he cooed.

"Nigga, close the door."

He chuckled, moving toward the door with me damn near clipping his heels. Then there was a flash, a bang, and a grunt.

My ears rang as I screamed, running through the open bedroom doorway and down the stairs in pursuit of the intruder while letting off shots. I was so damn discombobulated; I kept missing the motherfucker in the dark clothes. Me! I never missed. Never!

I stopped short of following him as he sprinted out the back door because I had more important business to attend to.

As I raced back up the stairs, I realized I was still nude. So was Bo as he lay on the floor with blood oozing from the hole in his chest.

36

Everything was fuzzy except for the pain. The pain was suffocating me, or maybe it was the blood. Either way, I couldn't breathe. Memphis was gone, probably pursuing the motherfucker who shot me.

I coughed as my mind raced with thoughts. Who, what, why, and where? Who did this, or better yet, who hired them to do this? The field of possible suspects was wide open. What did I miss to not see this coming? Why the fuck didn't he take the head shot? I damn sure would have. Where was my got damn security?

I coughed again and closed my eyes. I was tired as hell. Tired and cold but the bullet felt so damn hot. I was still suffocating, too.

Shit, I'm going to die, I thought, and I was selfish enough to be happy I was going before she did. I just couldn't take losing her.

Ever.

Then I heard her voice, her words coming like a flood—rushed and forceful. Something about an ambulance coming. Something about me opening my eyes. So, I did, taking in every inch of her face while recalling every inch of her body at the same time. There was so much shit I needed to tell her, like how she was my dream come true. I wished I could tell her it was okay for me to die because I got her back. I *finally* got her back, and she loved me again. I wanted to say that I loved her one last time, but when I opened my mouth, I couldn't speak. It was full of blood.

"Fuck! They need to hurry the hell up!" she said, sounding mad as hell. This was her version of panicking.

She was holding my hand, and I managed to squeeze it, my eyes fixed on her face before everything...went black.

37

Memphis

I sat in the waiting area with a straight back, my eyes focused on the digital clock hanging on the wall above the information desk. He wasn't dead...anymore. The paramedics had to resuscitate him before bringing him here to the hospital where they rushed him into surgery. Lots of blood lost, an injured lung, severe hypoxia. They said he might even end up on a ventilator. I probably should've been sad or worried, but I was pissed.

Completely pissed.

"Got here as soon as I could. Your sister is mad I wouldn't let her come with me."

Ray.

I lifted my eyes to him. "Why'd you tell her?" I asked, my voice sounding monotone in my own ears.

"It's on the news, Memphis. Every damn station is talking about a home invasion and the local man who was shot. They've released Bo's name. I ain't had to tell her shit," he replied.

"Who the fuck leaked his name? Shit!"

"Don't know. What you need me to do? Finish him off? I got scrubs and everything. I can get the twins to work on disabling cameras—"

"I need you to help me find out who did this."

In my periphery, I could see him nod. "Okay, you wanna thank them or something? If you'd asked me, I woulda done it. Shit, I started to do it on my own, but I was tryna let you handle it."

I turned to face him, shaking my head. "He's a piece of shit in a lot of ways, but he's mine...for better or worse. I'm the only someone who has the right to kill him."

He frowned, blinked a few times, and sighed. "You still love the motherfucker. I mean, as twisted as all this shit between you and him has been, I can see that he has real feelings for you, too. I honestly thought you still hated him."

"I do."

"But you love him?"

"Listen, if this shit is on the news, his damn family will be here any minute. We don't have long to talk."

"Okay. What you need?"

"Fuck," I muttered upon seeing his mother, brother, and son rushing toward me. "Just stay with me for now. Later, we'll put together a plan to find out which one of these motherfuckers—" I nodded toward my in-laws. "—tried to have my husband killed."

∾

HIS MOTHER LOOKED HARRIED, like she'd just seen or heard a ghost. I almost believed she was worried about her son.

Heavy on the *almost*.

"Memphis, why didn't you call me to let me know what's going on with my boy?!" she shrieked, her arm looped with Tavares's. They and Zaccai were now standing over me.

"I don't have your number," I replied. The fact that I even answered her was a testament to how stressed I was because *fuck her*.

"Well, Bo does. Where's his phone?"

I lifted one of the two phones sitting in my lap. "Right here."

She stared at me, and I stared right back.

Finally, she asked, "You didn't think to use his phone to call me?"

"She probably doesn't have his passcode," Zaccai cut in with a smirk.

I ignored him and didn't bother to answer his mother. It was taking all my strength not to snap both their necks.

"I'm Ray Nation, Memphis's brother-in-law," came out of nowhere.

I glanced at Ray to see the glare he was shooting at Zaccai, who undoubtedly knew him. Zaccai still worked for The Agency, and I could see the absolute lust for power in his eyes now that his brother was down. He had me fucked up if he thought he was going to usurp my dominion.

Zaccai looked at Ray and led his mother away from us as she tried to say something else to me.

"You know Zaccai?" I asked Ray.

"He definitely knows me. I recognize his voice. He was my handler."

So that's what Bo had him doing? Damn, he didn't even put him in administration, but then again, I was sure he didn't trust Zaccai enough to give him a more elevated role.

Ray and I sat there in silence for a long while before he spoke again. "My money is on Zaccai being behind this."

With my eyes fixed on the clock again, I said, "Same. I just need proof. I don't wanna spill the wrong blood."

38

Memphis

He was out of surgery and on his way to the surgical ICU, according to the doctor, who also said things looked good. Barring some unforeseen complications, Bo was expected to make a full recovery. He was on a ventilator, but they were looking to start weaning him off it. Motherfucker was too damn evil to die.

Good. If him dying wouldn't be a worry, I'd have the bandwidth to kill Zaccai.

"So, he can have visitors?" Tavares asked.

I frowned, glancing at him to see concern in his eyes. Shit, maybe he *did* care about his father.

Nah.

"After they get him settled, they'll come out to the ICU waiting area and let you all know," the doctor replied.

I thanked him, and Ray and I made our way up to that waiting room.

My ass had barely hit the seat when Bo's mother appeared before me...again. Ray was in the restroom, so I supposed she thought she was safe with just me.

That's craaaaazy.

Without an invitation, she took the seat next to mine.

Sighing, I said, "Look—"

With lifted hands, she declared, "I come in peace. I apologize for the way I behaved earlier. I was worried about my son, and you were sitting there looking nonchalant. I think I forgot what kind of woman you are."

I looked at her. "And what kind of woman is that? Before you answer, just know I don't need a gun to fuck you up, and yes, I will fight an old bitch."

She blinked a few times before saying, "Tough. You're tough. You're also mean, and I suppose those attributes are what attracted my son to you. You are honestly a lot like me."

"No...I'm a lot of things, but I'm not evil. Sorry."

She smiled. "Neither am I. I'm merely a woman who believes in protecting what's hers."

"The only thing you care about protecting is your money, or rather, your access to *my husband's* money. That, plus your little ego."

"Touché. I do care about my family, too, you know? I love your husband, no matter what he might have told you."

"Lady, he ain't had to tell me a got damn thing. I've seen you in action, remember?"

"That...at the time, I believed his feelings for you would cloud his judgement. Bo was always so methodical. I'd never seen him like he was with you. I knew he'd give you anything."

"And he did. Sucks for you."

"No, I think you're an excellent choice to run The Agency with him."

"Mm-hmm." I lowered my voice and added, "If I find out you had anything to do with this, I'ma fuck you all the way up, and then I'll fuck Zaccai up for good measure. Get away from me and *stay* away from me. When they call for visitors, do not get your old ass up. You can see him when I leave."

She blinked a few more times before leaving just as Ray returned.

"You good?" he asked as he reclaimed his seat.

"I'm fucking perfect."

"Aw, shit. You ready for war for real."

"Yep. I just need to see him, and then we can get to work. The first thing I need to know is where the fuck his security is. Their base is across the street from our house. The split level one with the gray door."

"I can put the Gutierrez twins on that right now."

"Good. I'll get in touch with my team, too."

An hour later, I was informed that Bo could have visitors. When I saw his family members stand and begin walking toward me, I shot them a look that made them stop in their tracks. Ray went with me but hung outside the room while I entered it.

Bo's eyes were closed, and I took a minute to observe the monitors, IV poles, and IV bags. There was also a bag of blood. He was off the ventilator, but still, there were so many contraptions and tubes attached to him. I hated seeing his wicked ass like this. It would've broken my heart if I wasn't so damn angry.

His eyes popped open and quickly found me as if he'd sensed my presence. Emotion filled them as he visually surveyed me.

"I wasn't hit. I'm fine," I assured him.

He nodded, squeezing his eyes shut. "Come here, baby," he said, his voice weak and raspy.

I did, grasping his hand. In turn, he used his free hand to beckon me closer, and I lowered my head so that my lips nearly met his.

"You sure you okay?" he whispered.

"Physically, yes. Mentally? That's another story."

"You ready to fuck somebody up. I can see it on your face."

"Yeah, I am."

"My security?"

"I don't know what happened to them...yet."

He nodded.

"Hey, I don't want you to worry about that. Just get better."

"Look through the database. Get 75GL for backup. You can trust him. I don't..." he stopped, shutting his eyes for a moment, and when he spoke again, his voice was weaker. "I don't want you out there alone. Somebody gotta have your back."

"Bo, I got this. You need to rest. Stop worrying about me."

He nodded again, and when I pressed my lips to his, he moaned, his hand on the back of my head. My body tingled like it always did at his touch. It was a fucking shame how much I loved this man.

"I'll be back," I said. "Your family is outside. Do you want to see them?"

He slowly shook his head and said, "Hell no. Just you."

I didn't bother speaking to the Pierces when I left. I informed the nurses that they weren't to see him, and that was that. I didn't have time to argue with them.

~

"I could've driven myself," I said, my eyes on the windshield as Ray drove us to my house.

"Nah, you're fucked up, as you should be. I got it," Ray replied.

"Well, thanks for helping me."

"Aw, hell. Yeah, I made the right decision. If you being nice to me and shit, you definitely don't need to be driving."

"If my sister and nieces didn't love you, I'd shoot you right now."

He chuckled. "There she is...the *real* Memphis King."

"Mm-hmm."

His phone rang, and he answered it through the car's stereo system with, "Hola! What you got for me, Bruno?"

"We found the guys in the house across from the crime scene. Dead. One shot to the head each," came the heavily accented voice.

"Shit," I muttered. "How many did they find?" I asked Ray.

"¿Cuantos cuerpos?" Ray questioned the man.

"Dos," Bruno quickly replied.

Bells and whistles went off in my head as he ended the call. "Should've been three," I said more to myself than him. "All three were on duty last night. Either the third guy got away, or..."

"Or the third guy is the shooter," Ray finished.

"Yeah."

39

Memphis

"All these fucking reporters, and is that Umber's truck?" Ray asked as he pulled into my driveway. I'd been so far up in my head that I didn't even notice her truck. Then again, the reporters and their vans were a valid reason to have missed it. I hated this shit. The issue was that this was a quiet neighborhood in the suburbs. Nothing ever happened here...until it did.

"Of course it is. Who else do we know with a dusty-ass pickup truck?" I replied.

Ray laughed. "Leave Umber alone. If we ever need to survive in the wilderness and shit, we got us an expert."

I shook my head. "I really don't have time to pretend I'm not a killer right now. She shouldn't be here."

"I know, but she's probably just worried about you. Damn, am I really the voice of reason right now?"

"It would seem so because it ain't shit reasonable about what I wanna do right now."

"I feel you."

He'd barely put his vehicle in park before I hopped out of it, making quick strides to my front door while ignoring the shouted voices of the reporters.

"Mem! Wait!" Umber called, her voice ringing loud as she climbed out of her truck and trotted toward me.

Well, if the press didn't already know my name, they did now, or at least the abbreviated version of it.

I told myself not to snap at my baby sister. It wasn't her fault I was craving blood like a damn vampire. So, I took a deep breath and unlocked the door, turning to wait for her.

As soon as she reached me, she pulled me into a hug that I involuntarily leaned into.

"Lil told me what happened! Daddy is a wreck; you gotta call him! Are you okay? How is Bo?" she babbled.

By then, Ray was standing a few feet behind Umber, giving me an admonishing look.

Rolling my eyes at him, I told my sister, "I'm fine. Bo is doing okay. Come on inside," before backing out of her embrace.

I stepped into the mess the police had made of the house and wanted to scream. Then, I was reminded of the blood in our bedroom doorway.

I didn't realize I had blanked out until Umber spoke. "You shouldn't stay here."

Frowning, I focused on her. "What?"

"You don't need to stay here with the press and this being a crime scene and all."

I shook my head, trying to rid it of the cobwebs. "No, I mean, yeah. I'll...I still have the apartment."

My tall-ass little sister moved closer to me. "I don't think you should be alone right now. You can stay with me."

My eyebrows flew up. "Um, I ain't pissing and shitting in no outhouse, Umber."

She blew out an exasperated breath. "It's a composting toilet, and it's *inside* the house!"

"Nah, I'm good. There's security at my building, and the reporters won't be able to get in."

"What the fuck is a composting toilet?" Ray asked.

"So, it's a dry toilet. The waste is broken down by microorganisms into compost!" Umber excitedly explained.

"Yeah, you don't need to be alone, but you ain't gotta use one of them dry shitters, either. You can stay with me and Lilith. We won't ask you to babysit," Ray offered.

I started to protest but realized that was actually a good idea. It made for great logistics. So, I said, "Okay, I'll stay at the Nation house."

Umber threw up her hands. "Y'all *stay* hating on my place!"

"Damn, this was the shortest retirement in modern history," Jerryn quipped. "I saw that text saying you need me and damn near fainted. Management ain't working for you?"

Holding my phone to my ear with my shoulder, I activated the VPN on my laptop and logged into The Agency's database. "You seen the news?" I asked.

"You know I don't watch the news unless I'm on an assignment. I recently became unemployed, Raja. Remember?"

"Then that explains it. Someone entered me and Bo's house and shot him. I'm okay, before you ask. I pursued the shooter but couldn't stop them. Don't know who it was. They had on a ski mask and dark clothes. He or she shot him in the chest, but I think that's because they didn't expect him to be at the bedroom door. Probably planned on headshots while we were asleep. All our surveillance was disabled. Two of our security guards were shot dead. One is missing."

"Okay, you got a name for the missing one?"

"Yep. I already gave it to Montana. She's also going to hack into some of the doorbell cams and shit in the area. I need you to look into a list of people. Check out their bank transactions, text messages, phone calls. I need to see who set us up."

"But—"

"I know this is Montana's thing, but I need more than one person on this digital stuff, and you have resources that specialize in chatter."

"Raja, I love you, but I can't ask her to do this. We made a deal..."

"Jerryn, I wouldn't ask if I could avoid it. Someone shot my husband."

Silence, and then he said, "You really love him. You've always loved him," as if just realizing this truth.

"Jerryn, I know you and I...we shared something in the past, but—"

"Raja, I never expected you to feel for me what I felt for you. I always got that your heart was unavailable. It's just...he doesn't deserve you. You know that, right?"

"No, I'm no better than him. I realize you think I'm altruistic because of the targets I choose, but I'm still a killer. I've trained other killers. Neither him nor I deserve love, but we found it in each other. I...I need him."

He sighed into the phone. "It would be best if you asked her. She's always liked you."

"I'm down."

∿

TATIANA MCREYNOLDS WAS AN ABSOLUTELY gorgeous ebony-skinned woman with long limbs and a crown of soft-looking kinky hair. She was dressed elegantly in a white shift dress and bare feet, sitting on the sofa in the modern style home she and Jerryn shared. She greeted me with a smile and pulled me into a hug as I sat down beside her.

"So good to see you, Memphis!" she gushed. It was weird hearing her speak in her real accent after she'd used the fake American one for so many years.

"Good to see you, too. Jerryn told you about my predicament?" I asked.

"Da. Your husband was shot. You're trying to find the culprit."

I nodded. "And I need your help, your...expertise."

Her eyes drifted to her husband whom she obviously loved. I hated to mess up the little "don't ask, don't tell" agreement they made to save their marriage, but desperate times...

"I'm okay with it...for her," Jerryn assured her.

She returned her gaze to me. "Come. I'll help."

I followed her into her home office, a space that was off limits to Jerryn. I felt privileged to watch this woman work. Born and raised in Russia and highly perceptive, Tatiana was recruited by her home country's government to train and work in intelligence. She was sent to work in the US ten years ago, met and fell in love with Jerryn five years later. He pretended to be a software analyst while she pretended to be in data entry. Of course, they both eventually figured out the truth and made the aforementioned agreement. So yeah, I was soliciting help from an actual Russian spy who was planted in my country to fuck it up.

A means to an end and all that shit.

"All these people are related to your husband?" she asked as she tapped away at her computer's keyboard.

"Correct."

"Crazy family?"

"The craziest."

She giggled as her elegant fingers continued to work.

I watched her until a text from Lilith came through: *How you spend the night and leave this morning without saying good morning or bitch, fuck you or something?*

I didn't answer.

"This will take a while, but I will get the information you need. You can stay or I can send it to you. You have ProtonMail, TorBox, something like that? Oh! The Agency has its own host?"

"It does, but I'll wait."

She shrugged. "Okay."

I'm not sure how much time had passed or how long I'd been sleeping in that chair in Tatiana's office when she shook me awake and informed me that she was done, but I was rested enough to sit at her computer and begin loading the information onto the external drives I'd brought with me, and then I left, hoping I hadn't fucked up my friend's marriage while trying to save mine.

40

Memphis

Jerryn met me at Ray's and Lilith's fortress of a house about an hour later. He seemed cool, so I supposed everything was good with him and Tatiana.

Holed up in Ray's safe room, he, Jerryn, and I spent hours upon hours with few breaks going through the volumes of intel Tatiana mined—emails, dark web emails, texts, phone calls...hell, she'd even retrieved data from burner phones pinging at the Pierce mansion.

We hadn't found shit.

"Whichever one of them did it covered their tracks like a mother-fucker. You heard back from your hacker about the surveillance or the missing bodyguard?" Ray questioned. "What you say his name is?"

I frowned. "Jafar O'Connor, but that could be an alias."

"Gotta be," Jerryn interjected.

"And as a matter of fact, I *haven't* heard from her, which is strange," I continued. "Let me call her." Picking up my phone, I realized why I hadn't heard from her. "No signal."

"Shit, my bad. I thought I turned that thing off," Ray said, leaving to move deeper into the safe room and returning with a device I recognized as a cell phone jammer. "Just bought this one. An upgrade. I was playing around with it earlier."

"What the hell you need with that? You ain't in the field no more," I pointed out.

"I mean...just in case," he said, wearing a sheepish grin as he switched the jammer off.

Instantly, all three of our phones resurrected with beeps and buzzes. Sure enough, I'd received several messages from Montana asking me to call her. There was also a voicemail from the hospital. Bo's condition had declined.

THERE WERE a lot of thoughts in my head as I rode to the hospital in silence, the loudest being: *I shouldn't have left him.*

I really shouldn't have, but once I saw that he was stable, I went into the mode most comfortable for me. I became laser focused on seeking revenge, killing, blowing off steam the best way I knew how when I should've been by his side like he'd been by mine throughout my ordeal with Polycythemia Vera.

I was a shitty fucking wife.

"Get out your head blaming yourself. You thought he was good.

You did what came natural and got to work," Ray said, knowing me way too well.

I nodded, glancing over at my sister's husband. "I hear you, but what if it was Lilith in the hospital? Where would you be right now?"

"With her, but we ain't got the same history as you and him," he replied.

"The history is we've loved each other most our lives, together or apart, and instead of sitting in that hospital and seeing him every chance I could, I went on a fucking killing mission."

"It's in you. It's in me, and I fight that shit every day. You wanna stop it from being a reflex? Fight that shit. One thing I know is you're good at fighting."

I chuckled. "That's the truth."

"And so is he. A nigga in his position shoulda *been* gone, but he ain't. He'll make it."

I nodded, fixed my eyes outside the passenger window, and hoped Ray was right.

We were in our backyard. I was on the grill while my wife sat and watched me the way she always did when she thought I wasn't paying attention—with real love in her eyes. I smiled to myself because while any hate she once or still held for me was real, so was the love.

We had a love so strong that it literally stood the test of time, a love so strong that years of separation couldn't weaken it. All we needed was a chance. I'd always known that was all it would take. I always knew if I could just touch her, hold her in my arms again, the time apart would mean nothing.

"The shrimp are done, baby," I said, observing the skewers on the grill. "Bring me something to put them in."

No response.

I turned to see that she was gone. The back door was closed. It was almost as if she'd never been there, and I inexplicably panicked. Was I losing my mind? Was she *ever* here?

"Baby!" I yelled.

Nothing.

"King!"

Still, nothing.

Dropping the long fork I held, I took off for the house, bursting through the back door. "Baby! You in here?!" Silently, I pleaded, *please be in here.*

"I'm right here, baby," she said, coming from the direction of the bathroom located between the kitchen and living room. "I'm right here."

Relief flooded me as I moved closer to her, yanking her into a hug.

"You missed me?" she crooned.

"Yeah...yeah," I breathed.

41

Memphis

"You missed me?" I softly asked as I sat in a chair next to his bed, rubbing his dry hand.

His chest tube—whatever the-fuck that was—had become clogged with blood clots, per the doctor. This caused Bo's injured lung to collapse, which led to him having trouble breathing, and now, he was back on the ventilator. I was...I'm not sure. I suppose I was somewhere between blindingly angry and utterly shattered.

So much time wasted. So much time wasted hating him. So much time wasted wanting him. Now, I had him, and some motherfucker was on the brink of taking him away from me.

Life was such a rigged game.

Resting my head on the mattress beside Bo, I worked to convince myself not to charge out of the hospital and into his mother's house to shoot up the entire family. It took A LOT of work.

"Bo, I know you can hear me. I just...I feel like...shit." Since my words were failing me, I closed my mouth and sat there in silence. It was all I could do.

"You taking care of yourself? I know that's your husband, but you got your own health to think about, baby girl," my daddy said into the phone.

"I'm fine," I replied as I paced the little snack room adjacent to the ICU waiting area. "I went downstairs to the lab for my scheduled phlebotomy this morning. I'm taking my aspirin. Resting as best I can. Not feeling bad or anything."

"Well, you sound tired."

"I'm not," I lied.

"Uh-huh...Memphis, what is that man into to get shot like that in his own home? That's a good neighborhood y'all living in. Stuff like that don't happen out there."

I sighed, stopping in my tracks for a second before resuming my pacing. "He works in corporate. He's not into anything." Another necessary lie.

"Mm-hmm, I don't know what I did for you and Lilly to fool with these types of men. I would say be careful, but knowing you, I need to warn whoever shot him instead."

That made me smile. "Daddy, I gotta go. Love you."

"Love you more, baby girl."

No sooner than that call ended, one came through from Montana.

"Hey," I answered, "I'm sorry I haven't returned your calls or messages. I had to rush back to the hospital a couple days ago and—"

"No worries. Jerryn filled me in on everything. I thought I'd give you a day or two before calling again," she said.

"Thanks. So...what's the word? Anything on the bodyguard?"

"Yes! Finally!" she chirped. "But first...how is hubby?"

"He's...I don't know."

"Yeah. So...Jafar is an alias or *was* an alias."

"Shit, he's dead?"

"Yes. His real name was Nealy Watts."

"Damn, that ain't no better than the alias."

"I know, right? Anyway, he was twenty-nine, a Detroit native, and he was found dead in a hotel in Parkton. Um, the Starlight Hotel. Drug overdose."

"Hmm, Bo wouldn't have hired a drug addict. Somebody was done with him, so they disposed of him."

"Looks like it."

I blew out a breath. "I take it he has no connections to any of the Pierce family?"

"No overt connections, but I'll keep digging."

"Okay, thanks. Be sure to pass this along to Jerryn. He'll fill Ray in."

"Already done!"

42

Memphis

After a week, he was weaned off the ventilator again, and when I walked into the room to see him during the next visiting time, he was alert, greeting me with a wide grin.

If I was a crier, I would've dissolved into a puddle of tears right then and there. Instead, I rushed to his bedside and rained kisses all over his face.

"You look so much better! I could suck the skin off your dick right now," I whisper-screamed.

He softly chuckled, "I'd rather you sat that pussy of yours on my face."

43

I was finally moved to a regular room a few days after they took that damn tube out of my throat, and my first request was to meet with the team Memphis had assembled—Ray and Jerryn with Montana on the phone—after Jerryn swept the room for bugs, of course. Memphis didn't contact the Italian like I asked her to, so I did, and he was posted outside my door since it would be easier to access me on this unit.

Memphis and her team filled me in on what they'd found, which was nothing, and I could sense their shared frustration.

"My family ain't no slobs. It doesn't surprise me that they would cover their tracks. I *am* a little fucked up about the rogue security nigga. I had all kinds of checks done on him, on all of them," I said, my hand on my wife's thigh as she sat beside me on the bed.

"Yeah, Montana found all that fake background stuff for his alias. She said it was top tier work," Jerryn shared.

"And my folks are top tier. How the fuck did they miss this?" I mused aloud.

"Montana is a cut above the rest," Memphis informed me. "Not too many folks can touch her skills."

"Well, shit...she need to be on my payroll, then," I said.

"Facts," Ray agreed.

Memphis's phone buzzed and she groaned. "Umber's on her way up. We better wrap this up."

"No prob," Jerryn said. "I'll be in touch."

As he left the room, Memphis followed him, saying, "Let me run to the restroom. Be right back, Bo!"

"Okay, baby," I replied.

That left me and Ray, who held his seat, his eyes fixed on me.

"Damn, you look like you wanna finish the job," I pointed out.

He slowly nodded. "Oh, I do, but out of respect for your wife and mine, I won't."

"Okay...I can appreciate that. I also appreciate you helping her figure this shit out."

He shrugged. "She's family, was long before I married her sister. Most days, I can't stand her, but she's good people. You and your family just did to her what you've done to a lot of good folks."

I smirked. "You included, huh?"

"Nah, I know I ain't shit. I deserve whatever I got coming to me. Memphis, though? She's good at this shit. The best, actually, but she shouldn't be in this business, and you know it."

I nodded. "You're right, she never deserved this life, and hell, I don't deserve *her*. Think what you want, but I love her, and that's real."

"I can see that, but don't hurt her again. I am *not* playing with you."

"I ain't tryna lose her. Last thing I'ma do is hurt her."

He stood to leave. "Good."

"And Ray?"

"Yeah?"

"I might be down right now, but I ain't no punk. Don't forget that."

He gave *me* a smirk and left.

Fucking hot head.

"Hey!" Umber shrieked, pulling me into a hug. She was passing the unit's restroom as I exited it.

I jumped. "You scared the shit out of me. Hey, though."

She laughed. "Crazy timing, right?"

"Yeah. What's that?" I asked as I led her to Bo's room.

Holding up the bag she held, she said, "Some vegan soul food. I know you're trying to eat healthy now, and no, I didn't cook it."

"Thank God," I mumbled.

"I heard that," she uttered.

"You heard what?"

She rolled her eyes at me as we entered Bo's room.

"Look who's here," I said to Bo.

He looked up and smiled. "Hey, Umber. Here to see if my old ass is still kicking?"

Umber laughed. "That, and I wanted to feed your wife."

Bo's eyes softened. "I appreciate that. I've been worried about her."

I frowned. "Uh, you're the nigga who got shot. You have no business worrying about me."

"Worrying about you *is* my business. Always has been," Bo said.

We locked eyes for a moment, and I swear I'd all but forgotten Umber was in the room with us until she sang, "Awwwww!"

Glaring at her, I fussed, "Girl, shut up."

"WHY YOU TRYNA WALK SO FAST? You should've let me get a wheelchair. They got a couple in the lobby. So fucking stubborn," I hissed as we rode the elevator to my apartment.

"I been out the hospital for less than an hour and you ain't stopped talking crazy to me yet," he said, wearing a stupid grin on his face.

"Because you keep saying and doing dumb shit. First, you tried to drive. Then, you wanted to carry your ass back to the scene of the crime and let the damn Italian protect you all on his own instead of staying in my apartment."

"Protect *us*."

"Whatever. After all that, you damn near ran through the lobby, and now you're on this elevator out of fucking breath."

He coughed. "No-I-ain't."

"I swear you are a child."

He shrugged, still grinning.

Since he wanted to get on my damn nerves, I exited the elevator as soon as the doors slid open, leaving him behind. If his ass fell, at least I wouldn't see it.

"Now who's walking fast?" he said as he followed me to my door.

"Hmph," I muttered.

"That ass looking good enough to bite, though. I'm loving the view."

Trying to ignore his goofy ass, I unlocked the door, opened it, and was instantly accosted from behind. Bo's arms were around me, his harsh breath on my neck as the door slammed shut behind us. His dick poked me in the ass, and my pussy instantly cried out for help.

"Oooooo, shit! W-wait, Bo! The-the-the Italian is on his way up with your flowers and shiiiiit!"

"Mmmm, mm-hmm," he said into my neck.

Then his hands were on my breasts, squeezing them through my shirt and I found myself leaning into him because shit, he was *him* and I'd missed this. I'd missed this particular touch from him. This brand of closeness. This...heat. With the fact that we still didn't know who tried to have him killed and the truth that they might try again looming over us, I was honestly beyond eager to slide my pussy all over his body.

On gang.

He let me go, spinning me around and just...staring at me, his eyes seemingly taking in every inch of my face before settling on my lips.

"I look at you, and I think I know what Helen of Troy must've looked like. You are a world class beauty and don't think I don't know how lucky I am to have you in my life."

I felt my eyes mist, told myself to pull it together, and quickly moved in, crushing my mouth to his. From that point, things escalated so quickly that we were both naked when my doorbell rang.

"Yo, Boss!"

The Italian.

Lifting his mouth from mine for a brief moment, Bo called, "Leave everything by the door out there. We'll get it!"

"Ten-four!" the Italian yelled in response.

Then, mouth on mouth, tongues warring, hands roaming, I gently pushed him onto the couch, straddled him, and moaned when he lowered his head and nibbled at my right nipple, his hands tightly gripping my ass. I grinded against his thick erection, my pussy weeping all over it.

"Fuck, baby. You so damn hot. I need to be inside you," he whined as he moved his mouth from my breast to my chin.

Fighting to breathe steadily, I lifted from his lap to guide him inside me, slowly sliding down his hardness with a low, agonizing groan. He felt so good. Always had and always would because it was more than his length and girth. It was more than his hardness. It was him, *all* of him—his scent, his energy, his absolute and unequivocal love for me and mine for him.

Yeah, I loved the shit out of him.

While I rode him nice and easy, my walls gripping him with each stroke, he held my hips and stared into my eyes in amazement.

As ecstasy wrapped around us, blocking out everything else in the world, I told him, "I love you...I love you...I love you."

"I...love...you...too," he murmured as he closed his eyes and let his head fall against the top of the couch.

44

I know her pussy had to be tired, but I couldn't stop. I couldn't stop fucking her, touching her, tasting her, and as I sucked on her clit, the sound of her wails coupled with her wiggling beneath me made my damn heart sing. Pleasing her, knowing I could dismantle her with my body, was like a badge of honor for me. My wife wasn't shit to play with and she damn sure wasn't easily shaken, but me and my dick had her shook like a motherfucker.

"I fucking hate you! Oh, shit! I'ma cum right nowww!" she screamed.

"Mmmm..." I hummed against her pussy.

I liked to feel her cum, so when I felt her body stiffen after a couple more swipes of my tongue, I slid my fingers inside her and smiled when her pussy squeezed them. Once she calmed down, I kissed every inch of her pussy and then inched up her body to kiss her lips, a chaste kiss that soon evolved into me sharing her sweet flavor with her.

A few moments later, as she lay in my arms, she said, "I think we should go ahead and kill Zaccai."

"Why you say that? You sure it's him now? What changed? New intel?" I questioned her.

"No new intel. He's just the most logical choice. Even if your mother is behind it, she'd most likely enlist Zaccai. He's in the business. He knows how to execute a hit, no matter how lame he is."

"Right. So, Tavares is out? My ex-wife, too?"

"Tavares doesn't have enough sense to pull this off. Your mom has him too spoiled. Plus, he's a hot head and not very deliberate. Your ex-wife isn't exactly action oriented unless it involves illicit dick, from what I can tell."

"True...true. So, we kill Zaccai. I'm down with that. His ass needs to go, regardless. We can make it look like an accident. Only question is...when?"

"As soon as possible."

Memphis

Bo RECEIVED a ton of flowers once they moved him to a regular room. It seemed a lot of people admired my evil husband due to his philanthropy. Imagine that. There were bouquets and cards from several charities and a couple politicians, including the mayor.

Ho'.

I hadn't forgotten the dick lust that was in her eyes when she saw him at her party.

Anyway, I'd decided to get rid of the dried-out flowers when I saw it, the little card hidden within the huge arrangement of white hydrangeas. I mean, I'd noticed the card before but never bothered to read it after Bo said they were from the mayor.

Lifting the card from its little clear, fork-like holder, I scanned the message:

So glad you're doing well. Sending healing vibes and blessings to you. Much love.

Her name was signed at the bottom of the little card. I read it again and again, and then I went to my bedroom to wake my husband from his nap.

45

Memphis

Since he insisted on tagging along, Bo and I sat in the car staring at the video feed on my phone. My blood boiled, and my mind raced as we waited.

"I don't know how I missed this shit. I can't believe it," he mumbled for the fiftieth time.

"I missed it, too. Never crossed my mind," I said absently. I was ready to get this shit done. I just needed Montana to do her magic with the surveillance and alarms.

"But you *did* catch it. You figured it all out."

I lifted my eyes from my phone and looked at his pouting ass. "You mad I'm smarter than you, Mr. Pierce?"

Turning his head to look out the window, he said, "Fuck you. I hope a damn possum jumps out these woods and attacks your long head ass."

I laughed so hard that tears welled in my eyes, but my mirth was interrupted by Jerryn's voice in my ear: "Raja, we have an issue. You see this?"

Holding a finger to the earpiece, I said, "What happened? I'm looking at the video feed of the mayor's house right now, and..." I lost my words as I returned my attention to the phone where I could see a group of people, some in suits and others in casual clothes with FBI emblazoned on their jackets, approaching the front door of Mayor Shari Watts-Young's house. One of the suits was my sister... Umber.

The feds were raiding the mayor's house, and my sister was with them. I'd never seen her in anything other than a jogging suit. Where'd this motherfucker get real clothes from?

"What's going on?" Bo asked. He was connected to comms, too, so he'd heard Jerryn.

I felt him move in closer to me and knew he was seeing what I saw when he said, "The hell is she doing there with the Feds? Wait..."

His voice trailed off, and my mind stuttered. My sister planned hikes and killed wildlife and foraged for dandelions and shit. My sister lived in a cabin with her dog and pissed in a dry toilet. I was waiting to ambush the mayor's house because her maiden name on that card led me on a search that revealed Nealy Watts, Bo's would-be assassin, was her cousin. That information led to us uncovering her plot to eliminate the one person who had the type of dirt on her to ruin her congress bid—the man she hired to kill her husband whose death catapulted her political career. Once we had the correct target, it was easy for Montana to unearth the proof. But...

Umber was there because she was a federal agent?

Nah, couldn't be. There had to be some other explanation.

All doubt was erased when Umber, who seemed to be in the lead, flashed her credentials. Either Umber was a fed, or she was doing a damn good impression of one.

46

Memphis

S hit.
   Damn.
   Mother. Fuck!

47

Memphis

We left our spot in the woods less than a mile from the mayor's house and drove back to our apartment in silence, but I was sure Bo's thoughts were just as noisy and active as mine.

The quiet continued once we were home. The implications of this new knowledge were great. Bo and I were criminals. Hell, I was technically a serial killer. My sister was a federal agent. What the fuck? And how the fuck? As in, how the fuck did I not know this?

"You were too busy watching your own back and trying not to get caught to see it," Bo said, as if reading my mind. "And she's good. Very good. I couldn't see it, either."

"Yeah..."

"Plus, y'all avoid her home like the plague."

"And do! She knew we would. Me and Lil are too bougie. Hell... Daddy, too. Damn, she really is good. You think she knows?"

"About The Agency? Probably."

"Yeah."

"Baby—"

"I can't kill my sister. I can't let anything happen to her. I mean that. I don't want a hair on her head harmed."

He turned over in the bed to face me with a frown. "Don't you think I know you well enough to know that? Besides, if she knows and hasn't dimed us out or arrested us herself, that speaks volumes."

"It does." I sighed heavily. "I need to talk to her. Shit, we all do—me, you, Ray, Lilith. Fuck!"

"I agree, but not now. Not tonight. We rest tonight, and tomorrow, we talk to Umber about everything, including why the feds were at Shari's house."

"Shari, huh?"

"Baby, don't start. Her pussy wasn't even that good."

"What you mean it wasn't *that* good? It was good, though, huh?"

"You want me to eat your pussy or something? Would that help that damn attitude?"

"Yep."

In response, he slid down my body and snatched my whole soul from me.

Asshole.

THE FAMILY, sans Daddy and his wives, met at Ray's and Lilith's place under the guise of planning a family dinner. If I thought I was shocked, poor Lilith looked like she'd seen a whole convention of ghosts when Bo and I arrived early.

While our husbands huddled in the kitchen talking, I sat with Lilith on the living room sofa while Blaze and Katana played on the floor with their dolls.

"Should they be here for the meeting?" I asked her, my eyes on the cute little girls. Blaze's mean ass was frowning, as per usual.

"Uh, yeah. I mean, no. Shit, let me take them to Valentina. My head is everywhere," Lilith rambled before grasping both girls' hands and leading them out of the room.

When she returned and plopped down beside me, I said, "Yall really lucked out with Valentina. The girls seem to love her."

Lilith nodded, wringing her hands in her lap. "Yes, she's a great nanny. Mem, are we going to have to kill Umber? I can't take that."

With a furrowed brow, I replied, "We? You make one kill, and you think you're Colombiana or something?"

"Memphis!"

"No, girl! We are not killing our sister. I told Bo that was *not* happening."

"Yeah, I told Ray the same thing, but what are we going to do? What if she arrests all of us? Shit, I can't take that, either."

"I feel you. She sure took the mayor down. Racketeering, money laundering, shit's all over the news, although they didn't show Umber."

"Thank goodness they didn't. Daddy would have a stroke. Hey, Mem...do you think everything will be okay?"

I sighed, not wanting to lie, while at the same time, not wanting to alarm her. "I—"

"Umber's here. Just let her in the gate," Ray interrupted me.

Lilith grabbed my hand. "Shit."

⁓

UMBER WAS WEARING a black pant suit, and that? *That* made my stomach plummet into the depths of my ass. The no-nonsense look on her face didn't help, either. My only solace was that she was alone, but still...fuck!

We were all silent—me and Lilith still on the sofa, our men standing on either side of us, and all our eyes were on Umber perched on an accent chair.

"Well?" Umber finally said. "I take it the family dinner thing was a ruse. So...let's get this over with."

"Okay...when you start wearing pant suits?" I spoke up.

She smiled. "That is not what you want to ask."

I sighed. "To be honest...I'm scared to ask what I really want to ask."

"*You're* scared? Damn. Okay, I'll make it easy for you," Umber said, standing and reaching into her pants pocket to unearth an FBI badge and ID, placing both on the coffee table between us. "Now that that's out of the way, I also know what you do for a living—all of you."

"Oh, Lord!" Lilith whimpered.

Hell, I felt like putting on some sackcloth and gnashing my teeth because...damnit!

Ray and Bo groaned, "Shit," almost simultaneously.

"When did this happen? You being an agent, I mean. Why didn't you tell us?" I probed.

"I've been with the bureau in some capacity for thirteen years. I didn't tell you all because I didn't want you to worry," she explained.

"Thirteen years?!" Lilith screeched.

Umber nodded.

"I...why would we be worried? I taught you how to fight. I know you can take care of yourself," I said.

"I'm your baby sister. You telling me you wouldn't have worried at all?" she inquired with a smirk.

I shrugged. "Maybe a little."

"Mm-hmm, and once I got past that concern, I didn't want you to worry about me arresting you," she said all matter-of-factly.

My mouth dropped open. "W-what?"

"The bureau knows about The Agency, *everything* about it. We're one of your clients."

48

Memphis

"Wait, what?" Bo blurted. "What did you say?"

"The bureau has hired The Agency many times to eliminate threats to our country. Of course, we use aliases," Umber explained.

"Uh..." I mumbled.

"For instance, Judge Baxter? Us."

"I...what?" I stammered because...huh?

"Therefore, The Agency is a protected entity. I couldn't arrest you all even if I wanted to. I don't want to, by the way."

"That means...all this time, you knew?" I asked.

"That you were an assassin? No. I knew you didn't give a damn about a facial, though. You picked the world's worst cover," Umber advised me.

"You ain't lying about that," Lilith agreed.

"Fuck both of y'all," I gritted.

"Anyway, I figured it out a while back. I noticed a gun at your ankle sometimes. Plus, you give off murdery vibes," Umber continued.

"Wow," I said.

"And I know about Ray and Bo. I also know you lowkey frisked me when I arrived today, Ray, and that you're using a cell phone jammer right now," Umber shared.

"Damn, I was hugging you, not frisking you, sis-in-law," Ray lied.

"Nigga, please," Umber retorted.

"So...you don't be hiking and picking weeds?" I asked.

She rolled her eyes. "I do hike and *forage*, but catching bad guys is what pays the bills."

"Damn, if Daddy only knew about his girls," Lilith mused.

"Right," I said.

EPILOGUE

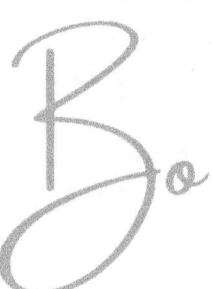

There we were again—my wife and I on one side of the table, my family on the other. Tavares and Zaccai flanked my mother, and Layla sat holding Zaccai's hand, her new engagement ring glistening. My brother had finally popped the question. Those two were a match made in Hades for sure.

We were at the company compound for a meeting I'd called. My new security members were stationed throughout the building and outside on the property.

"First, thank you all for coming," I began.

"Of course. We wouldn't miss it. I...uh, you look good. I hate this is my first time seeing you since you were injured," my mother expressed.

I shrugged. "Had to be careful. Wasn't sure who I could trust other than my wife."

She nodded. "And you believe you can trust me now?"

"No, but I do know you didn't try to kill me. We found the people behind that."

"Good. I take it you all handled that in-house. I see the police are still calling your shooting unsolved."

"Yeah, well...let's get on with the meeting. Baby?" I said, deferring to Memphis.

My beautiful wife squared her shoulders and fixed her eyes on my family. "First, I want to talk about recruiting some new agents. I think we should take it back old school like when I was brought on. We need operatives monitoring self-defense classes..."

I watched her work and hoped she was right about not shutting my family out of the business. She believed that was the best thing to do to protect The Agency, and I trusted her insight completely. She was the only reason my family was still alive, having advised that killing them all would more than likely compromise The Agency. When I suggested just offing my mom, she rejected that, too, pointing out that my mom kept everyone else in line.

She was right, and I hated it.

An hour later, Memphis had wrapped up the meeting when my mother said, "Well done, Memphis."

"Thank you," my wife answered curtly.

"I'd love to meet your family. You know, I'm a fan of your father's music. We should plan a gathering soon."

Memphis smiled, placing a hand on her hip. "With all due disrespect, *hell no*. Business is business. That's all this is and all it'll ever be between me and you."

Tavares and Zaccai looked like they wanted to say something but didn't. Good, because my gun was always ready. Yeah, I'd agreed to let them live, but I didn't mind asking for forgiveness.

SHE WAS SO beautiful standing before me in a see-through orange dress and nothing else, her red-painted toenails digging in the sand. No words passed between us, just my eyes raking over the glory that was her body and hers observing my assessment.

Love.

I never deserved it but was beyond fortunate to have hers. Actually, this had to be a fluke or glitch in the damn matrix because Memphis Blue King-Pierce was everything and beyond. Beauty, brains, and a pussy that could make nations of men fall to their knees.

She smiled, slowly making her way to me. I sat up in the lounger, watching as she leaned in to kiss me before straddling my lap. Settling onto me, she rubbed a finger over the raised scar on my chest, a landmark and reminder of a major near miss. Then she kissed it before locking eyes with mine.

Giving her a lopsided grin, I said, "Damn, you being all sweet and gentle and shit. This an anniversary thing or something?"

Smirking, she lifted from my lap, pulling the dress over her head. My hands instantly moved to her breasts as she reached down to free my dick from my shorts.

"After a whole year of being your wife, I figured the least I could do is be halfway nice to you, but if you say some more dumb shit, I'ma stop."

I chuckled. "Heard. Hey, I love you."

As she slid down on my steel, she whimpered, "I love you, too," and there on the beach of our familiar Zanzibar oasis, we made love as the sun ducked beneath the ocean.

ABOUT THE AUTHOR

A true southern girl, Audie Award-nominated author Alexandria House has an affinity for a good banana pudding, Neo Soul music, and tall Black men in suits. When this music-loving fashionista is not shopping, she's writing steamy stories about real Black love.

Connect with Alexandria!

ALSO BY ALEXANDRIA HOUSE

The Love After Series

Higher Love

Made to Love

Real Love

The Strickland Sisters Series

Stay with Me

Believe in Me

Be with Me

The McClain Brothers Series

Let Me Love You

Let Me Hold You

Let Me Show You

Let Me Free You

Let Me Please You (A McClain Family Novella)

The Them Boys Series

Set

Jah

Shu

The Romey U Series

Teach Me

Touch Me

Temper Me

The St. Louis Cyclones Series

Flagrant

Technical

Personal

The St. Louis Sires Series

Goal

Holding

Assist

The Three Kings Series

Lilith

Memphis

Short Works

Baby, Be Mine

Merry Christmas, Baby

Always My Baby

Should've Been

All I Want

New Year, New Boo?

Sanctuary (Paranormal)

the exhibition

Jingle Mingle

Joonteenth

F*cking on the 4th

Schoolhouse THOT

Two Hearts

24/7

Short Story Collections

the love deluxe mixtape

the love galore mixtape

the love infinite mixtape

The Holiday Shorts

Poetry

The Book of Nyles

Text alexhouse to (833) 445-0326 to be notified of new releases.